Confederate

Contents

Preface

The Civil War is the favorite subject of alternative history discussions because it was such a close-run struggle that any number of deviations from actual events might have changed its outcome. This book addresses a question even larger than the war itself. What if the South had ***not*** seceded?

The pivotal event enabling the South's secession was the disruption of the Democratic Party during its convention in Charleston, South Carolina in March 1860. Alabama "Fire Eater" William Lowndes Yancey had made it his life's work to lead the South into secession and independence. To take the South out of the Union, he understood it would first be necessary to divide and destroy the Democratic Party that bound together the North and South. In 1860 events aligned in his favor and he succeeded in leading the delegates of fifteen Slave States out of the convention.

After its disruption in Charleston, the Democrats split into three factions --- a Northern faction headed by Senator Stephen Douglas of Illinois, a Southern Rights faction headed by John Breckinridge of Kentucky, and a "Constitutional Union" faction headed by John Bell of Tennessee.

In the election, the fragmented Democrats were beaten by Abraham Lincoln's united Republicans, who received an electoral vote majority while winning less than 40% of the popular vote. The vote was especially close in several Free States. In the four-way contest Lincoln won California with only 32% of the popular vote and Oregon with 36%. He barely prevailed in Illinois with 50.7% and in Indiana with 51.1%.

If the Democrats had not discredited themselves by dividing into three competing factions, could they have prevailed in those four states, giving Stephen Douglas the electoral vote majority?

Douglas was considered by many to be the more experienced candidate of wider national appeal who would know how to avoid civil war. Even with his party split into three factions, Douglas won Sangamon County, Illinois, Lincoln's home of twenty-five years. The three-way split is known to have cost Douglas the votes of people who preferred a Republican electoral victory to having the election decided by an unruly House of Representatives.

A vigorous campaign by a Democratic Party united under Stephen Douglas would surely have carried California and Oregon and may well have picked up the few thousand votes it needed to win Indiana and Illinois.

This book makes its pivot into alternate history by proposing a compact between Stephen Douglas and Jefferson Davis that unites the Democratic Party during its Charleston Convention. A few years after writing this book, I learned that Stephen Douglas did in fact offer this compact to Jefferson Davis in December 1860, after Lincoln was elected, and the South was already in the process of leaving the Union. By that time all efforts at compromise to save the Union were bound to fail.

What if Douglas had offered his compact to Southerners in March 1860 when there was still time to keep the Democrats together? What if the united Democrats had elected *their* Union ticket of Stephen Douglas and Jefferson Davis? There would have been no secession of the South. But what about the anti-slavery men in the North? Would the United States, now styled the "Confederate Union," still be *their* country?

1

Stephen Douglas Home, Washington City, April 24, 1860

Senator Stephen Douglas sipped his whiskey, allowing inebriation to work its effect of enhancing his charm. Tonight, he called upon all his powers of persuasion. His fellow Senator Jefferson Davis sitting across the table was a difficult case.

He looked Davis in the eye, enunciating every word slowly and clearly.

"If we allow our party to divide and make war against itself a Republican *will* be elected President. If Seward, Chase, or Lincoln is elected President our nation *will* divide and make war upon itself. Is that not the least desirable of all possible outcomes?"

Davis shifted uncomfortably. The accumulated infirmities of a strenuous life punctuated by illness had made his body sore and his demeanor stern. His right foot still ached from the bone fragments shattered by a Mexican musket ball during his battle-winning stand at Buena Vista back in '47 that brought him to national prominence.

And then there was Douglas who always discomfited him. As a temperate and reflective personality, Davis could not help but dislike his hard-drinking, boisterous, and ever-scheming host. He saw Douglas as a "silver-tongued Cicero," a polished orator who constructed his positions more on expediency than principle.

However, all who were acquainted with Douglas admired his unsurpassed skill in leading the raucous political factions of his party. Davis therefore guarded his words, replying critically, while keeping an even temper in his voice.

"You know as well as I that Southern Democrats have lost faith in the national party because they do not trust *you*. You solemnly promised that your doctrine of Popular

Sovereignty would protect, as lawful property, our slaves in the Territories. You revoked that promise as soon as it became inconvenient to your own ambitions. For that reason, you no longer have our confidence."

Douglas again sipped his whiskey. He'd been party to many great political compromises consummated over liquor. He regretted that Davis had asked for nothing stronger than minted tea. It was hard to charm a sober man. Davis had even refused his offer of a Cuban cigar, the one vice Davis cherished. Davis was clearly on his guard against allowing the aroma of fine food, liquor, and cigars in Douglas' richly furnished library to inebriate his judgment.

Douglas put down his drink, folded his hands on the table, and leaned forward, again looking directly at Davis.

"Popular Sovereignty is founded upon the animating principle of this Union: that slavery may be allowed into territories whose settlers are amenable to having it, but not into territories where it is opposed."

Davis shook his head and sighed in frustration.

"Wasn't *that* 'cold coffee?' It allowed the Abolitionists to seize Kansas before our people had a fair chance to stake their claims. It has emboldened them to become obnoxious and unyielding. Now they insult us in the vilest terms in Congress. They spirit away our slaves on their Underground Railroad. They scoff at the Fugitive Slave Laws. They threaten to murder slave owners who seek the lawful return of their property. They sent John Brown to incite our slaves to rise against us and murder our families in our homes. We have reports from all over the South of Abolitionists caught conspiring with our slaves."

He raised his voice in the closest thing to anger his controlled personality would allow.

"We cannot and will not remain part of a country whose Northern majority has declared war against us! We cannot and will not remain members of a party that joins with our enemies to destroy us! Why is that so difficult for you to understand?"

Douglas thought about challenging Davis' presumption of "Abolitionists conspiring with slaves all over the South." He knew those reports were fanciful. There had been only one John Brown, and he was hanged in Virginia. But what did it matter what he believed?

It only mattered what Southerners believed. They saw John Brown's raid and the other affronts as a declaration of war. They felt sufficiently provoked to leave the national Democratic Party, then go out of the Union if the Republicans beat the divided remnants of the party in November's election.

"I would rather die than see this country extinguished," Douglas finally replied, hoping to prompt Davis into answering in kind.

"You know I have never desired to break this Union," Davis responded on cue. "But I would sooner see the South vindicate its rights outside the Union than be degraded into the humiliating surrender of our rights within it!"

"Then we must strengthen the South's position within the Union so that your rights to acquire more Slave States will be assured," replied Douglas, relieved that Davis had responded as he hoped. "I am thinking of a way for us to accomplish that together."

Davis grimaced. *What do you have up your sleeve this time, you little grog-drinking, electioneering demagogue?*

Douglas manifested his expression of persuasive seriousness perfected in decades of political controversies. He spoke in a voice barely above a whisper, as if letting go of a cherished secret.

"I have learned from President Buchanan's Cabinet that Napoleon III, with the backing of Britain, has planned the conquest of Mexico. France will justify the intervention both as a recovery of debt and a measure necessary to restore civil government in Mexico. Once Napoleon has possession of the country he will never give it up. With Britain backing him, we will not be able to drive him out."

Davis nodded in reluctant agreement. "Many of us in the South felt it necessary to acquire all of Mexico in '48, to ensure their security and ours. Of course, the Yankees thought they knew better and blocked us from acquiring the better part of the country. So now the French and British are coming in ahead of us."

Douglas was relieved that Davis believed his story. Douglas *had* colored it a bit. It would be more accurate to say Napoleon III "contemplated" the conquest of Mexico rather than "planned" it. Douglas surmised Britain would back France, though he knew no evidence of it.

However, it was generally known that Napoleon III coveted Mexico as his seat of empire in the Americas. The European powers had a long history of invading Latin American countries under the pretext of collecting debts. So, the substance of the story ran generally toward the truth. Perhaps Davis had already heard it from his contacts in Buchanan's administration.

"We were proven wrong not to have annexed all of Mexico in '48," agreed Douglas. "Now we understand our error, and the necessity of correcting it. We must vindicate the Monroe Doctrine while bringing American civilization to Mexico. The South will gain a new territory for slavery as large as all of our existing western territories combined, and one you will not have to share with the Abolitionists."

"Congress, with its Northern majority, will never approve our intervention in Mexico, let alone its acquisition," countered Davis, as Douglas had anticipated. "We had to drag them kicking and screaming into the war in '46. Even then they would not allow us to obtain half of what we had just expectations of receiving. The Yankees would rather Napoleon have Mexico than us." He rolled his eyes. *The Yankees* ***would*** *prefer Mexico to become a province of Napoleon's Empire than to enter the United States as Slave States!*

Douglas downed another swig of whiskey. Thrusting both arms forward he answered in a whisper carrying the force of a shout.

"This time we won't have to depend upon the thumb-sucking Congress! We will ask the states to mobilize their militias and send them into Mexico. We will plead the case that the French threat from Mexico is so imminent as will not admit of delay. The militias of the Southern States will heed our call. After they have liberated Mexico, Congress will have no choice but to bring the country into the Union as Slave States!"

Again, Davis responded as expected. "That is a very tall promise, Senator. Our party is in its present state of distress because so many in the South believe your previous promises were lacking sincerity."

Douglas looked Davis squarely in the eye. "This promise is sincere because it ***has*** to be! Our party and our nation have been brought to the brink of disunion because past compromises have not been carried out in good faith by either party. We can't remain united if any more promises are broken."

Davis remained poker-faced. *Say something to convince me this is a serious plan, not another one of your harebrained schemes intended to defraud the South like Popular Sovereignty turned out to be.*

Douglas gestured emphatically. "Our acquisition of Mexico will be part of a Grand Compromise to restore permanence to our Union!" He paused for effect. "I expect the South to accept the restoration of the Missouri Compromise Line, relinquishing claims to slave territories north of 36-30. The Free States will agree not to interfere with slavery south of the line, including in the new states we will acquire from Mexico. After we have brought Mexico into our Union as Slave States, we will ask the British to sell us the Canadas. That will bring the Northern Expansionists, men like Seward, into our party. The Republicans and Abolitionists will never threaten us again."

Douglas showed his most persuasive face. "Wouldn't the South covet these fertile tropical lands more than the arid deserts of our western territories? Wouldn't your slaveholders prefer expanding their plantations while remaining in the Union? Wouldn't *you* like to assure these promises will be executed in the same good faith as they are made?"

Davis was surprised by the seriousness of the plan. Then a warning sounded in his mind. *He may be trying to trick me into playing along until he wins the election. What's to stop him from repudiating his promises after he wins? He has done that before with Popular Sovereignty.*

But the word "you" had grabbed his attention, as Douglas intended, conjuring up the vision of being a partner in a grand venture. Mexico would be the grandest acquisition since the Louisiana Purchase. His mind vividly recalled the Mexican War of '46, where his heroism elevated him to national prominence.

Davis leaned forward. "What is to be my role in this....design?"

"I am asking you to form a Compact with me to unite our party!" exclaimed Douglas. "We must not divide into Northern and Southern factions between separate candidates. The Compact will result in my nomination as President and yours as Vice President. That office will not preclude you from accepting field command of the state militias we will be sending into Mexico."

Davis' eyes widened and his pulse quickened. His mind's eye recalled his glories as a younger man, of marching through the great valleys of the Mexican high country between sunlit mountains by day with crystal clear dark-blue skies overhead; talking around the campfires of the army on the cool nights; and fighting bravely with comrades under withering fire. His memory filtered out the screams of terror of men being shot in battle and dying beside him, and the rasping coughs of men dying from pneumonia. He forgot that on cold mornings his right ankle still seared with pain from the wound he'd taken during his heroic improvised defense that turned the tide at Buena Vista. Only the memories of marches to battle with gallant comrades, and their cheers of victory through clouds of smoke and fire, filtered into his consciousness.

Oh, what glorious days, when I and the nation were young and vigorous! We have become tired old men now, with this incessant wrangling over slavery. Perhaps Douglas is right; if Mexico is destined to be conquered, does necessity not require that it should be by the rising American Union instead of the degenerating Europeans?

Douglas saw Davis leaning back in his chair and putting his hand on his chin, riveted by the proposal. *He's swallowed the hook, now I must land him!*

"After we have brought Mexico into our Union, I want you to unite the South behind my effort to annex the Canadas. Then we will acquire Cuba and Central America. Our Union will fulfill its Manifest Destiny of becoming coextensive with the Northern Continent, from the Isthmus of Panama to the regions of eternal frost! We will have Slave States and Free States to settle for another hundred years --- and no reason to make war among ourselves."

Douglas handed Davis his Letter of Compact. Davis rapped his knuckles on the table as he read it. It consisted of but three sentences pledging both men to unite in support of the party's nominee. The unwritten consequences of the letter went far beyond its brevity.

Douglas waited anxiously while Davis read and reread the letter, rapping the table all the time. Douglas was as much discomfited by Davis as Davis was by him.

Davis sees himself as a man of principle. That is always the trouble with him. He represents himself as a patriot who loves every inch of this country, North and South, East and West. Then in the next breath he insists the states are sovereign governments that may secede from the Union any time they please. He believes the Union to be as fragile as a rope

11

of sand, then ties himself in knots interpreting the Constitution in his convoluted way. He combines the absolute worst aspects of being a States Rights and a Union man!

Davis was indeed wrestling with these questions. Douglas was proposing to invade Mexico with Southern state militias without asking Congress to declare war. Even a slick-talking huckster like Douglas wouldn't be able to cajole the Northern majority in the House of Representatives to authorize this war. Douglas would claim that Texas and other Southern States must act on their own because the conquest of Mexico by the French posed "such imminent danger as will not admit of delay," though no principled man would be comfortable with that explanation.

"You know the Abolitionists will raise a commotion to rock the heavens, especially your 'friend' Mr. Lincoln," Davis said dryly. "He'll have every Abolitionist from Maine to Kansas marching in torchlight processions. Wouldn't surprise me at all to see the Black Republicans nominate him to be their president."

"He tried to keep us out of Mexico in '46," Douglas reminded him. "What did that get him? One term in Congress, and no chance of re-election. He's a has-been. I finished him off in the Senate election. So, let him talk. Once the fighting gets started, Americans will rally to the colors. They always do. The Abolitionists will either hold their tongues or take a beating."

Davis considered the point. New England anti-slavery men had raised a ruckus when President Jefferson had purchased Louisiana from France. Even Jefferson thought it unconstitutional to annex Louisiana, then a foreign country. He had done it anyway because he believed its possession was essential for America's security. Since then, other vast territories, including Florida, Texas, and the Mexican Cession of 1848, had been obtained by various degrees of military intervention opposed by anti-slavery men. But once the fighting started, most Americans had supported the cause.

"What will we do with the Mexicans?" Davis asked. "There are eight million of them, more than all Whites in the Slave States. They're divided into a class system of peons, landowners, and clergy." He hesitated a moment before bringing up his greatest concern. "The only thing uniting them is hostility to slavery. We'll have to forcibly remove them from the fertile lands our slaveholders desire. It will be difficult to inflict such hardships on a people who have never done us any harm."

12

Douglas maintained his composure with difficulty. *I knew it! Davis never cared about the Mexicans when Southerners wanted to annex the whole of it. Now I propose it, and he's going to spend the next three hours raising objections!*

"We'll teach the Mexicans to appreciate slavery, like we've done with our Indians," Douglas assured him. "Didn't we remove the Cherokees from their lands in Georgia, Tennessee, and the Carolinas? And look at them now. They're prospering as never before in their own Indian Territory, under the auspices of American civilization, with the labor of Negroes they bought from us. The Mexicans will be fine once they get used to owning Negroes. We'll take the best land for our plantations, leaving enough for the Mexicans to improve themselves. In ten years, they'll be as loyal to the South as the Cherokees."

Douglas fixed his most imploring gaze upon Davis. Now was the time to seal the Compact.

"Didn't we just agree that it was a mistake not to annex all of Mexico in 1848? Now we know we must acquire Mexico before the French take it over. We know that if we don't knock the wind out of the Southern Fire Eaters, they'll disrupt our National Democratic Party. Then the Black Republicans will elect **their** anti-slavery president. That's what Yancey, Rhett, and the rest of those damned Fire Eaters are angling for, isn't it? They want a Black Republican in the White House as a pretext to leave the Union. It's up to you to help me save the Union...from the Fire Eaters and the Abolitionists!"

Davis stared into Douglas' devious face.

That damned Douglas always does this. The Yankee Abolitionists are provoking the dissolution of the Union, now he says it's up to me to save it by endorsing his scheme to annex Mexico. Maybe it would be best if the South broke its ties with the Free States altogether and went off into an independent Southern Republic. We wouldn't have to put up with insolent Republican Abolitionists or duplicitous schemers like Douglas in our own party.

But if we leave the Union, we'd have the Douglas Democrats against us. Perhaps they would join the Abolitionists, and we would face a united Free State North. I must admit that Douglas has concocted a well-considered plan. If it works the way he thinks, it will unite our patriotic, expansion-minded men of all sections.

Davis sloshed the ice in his minted tea.

Now, the question becomes whether Douglas means to keep his end of the bargain. He has promised to make me his Vice President, and for me to assume personal command of the militia armies sent into Mexico. I can just imagine him pretending to have nothing to do with the scheme and telling our Yankee opponents: "How was I to know that crazy Jefferson Davis was going to call out the Southern militias and invade Mexico?"

Davis grimaced and chuckled simultaneously as he contemplated the outrageous and unashamed lack of principle in Douglas' character. Come to think of it, Douglas did have one unyielding principle: he was a patriot who'd devoted his life to preserving the Union and expanding it. Would that induce Douglas to keep his end of the bargain? He was surely correct in saying the preservation of the Union depended on it.

*This sounds **exactly** like the kind of scheme Douglas would concoct: giving us Southerners a wink and a nod to annex Mexico while telling the Yankees he opposes it; but if they acquiesce in letting the South have Mexico, he will get them the Canadas. Yes, this is **precisely** the kind of scheme Douglas revels in! I do believe he will do it!*

He looked up at Douglas. He reminded himself not to show excessive enthusiasm in closing the deal.

"I can think of no immediate objection to the substance of your design. Let me think on it thoroughly. May I give you my affirmation or rejection in three days?"

Douglas frowned. "There isn't time for that. The Southern Rights men are in full control of the Charleston Convention. They've elected Caleb Cushing chairman and put a majority of their men on the platform committee. They're going to break that convention up if we don't stop them now. I would like you to deliver this Compact to the convention and have it read to the delegates before the Southern Rights men destroy the party. It's best that you leave for Charleston tomorrow. Make your final decision when you get there. But I am telling you most earnestly that if we do not deliver this Compact, we will lose our party and our country."

Davis read the Compact a third time, examining every word.

"I request one change, then. Replace the words 'Union of States' with 'Confederation of States.' That will appeal to the sentiments of the Southern delegates."

14

Douglas thought about revising the wording as Davis had recommended. He decided not to cross out "Union" but rather to qualify it by inserting the word "Confederate" in front of it. He made the insertions then signed his copies and gave two of them to Davis to counter-sign and present to the convention if he so decided.

Davis read the revised Compact. When he saw "Confederate Union" he gave Douglas the look of affirmation. He waved for the servant and asked for a rare indulgence of Kentucky Bourbon. He felt a grave responsibility being lifted from his shoulders. Rather than dwelling on the dreadful consequences of secession and civil war he began to imagine himself leading a rejuvenated nation in expanding its territory to the north and south.

He sipped the spirits and felt its warmth go through his body. He raised his glass.

"Let's drink a toast to our glorious and perpetual Confederate Union!"

2

Charleston South Carolina, April 28, 1860

Afternoon Session of the Democratic Party Convention

William Lowndes Yancey of Alabama contemplated the speech he was about to deliver to the assembled Democrats. He wanted it remembered as one of the momentous speeches in history, for he intended it to mark the day of conception of the Southern Republic as a nation of the Earth.

As he gathered his thoughts, he surveyed the six hundred and thirty delegates on the crowded floor of the South Carolina Institute Hall. The galleries above them were packed with spectators. The windows of the great hall were open to a height of forty feet, showing a sunny blue sky and letting in a fresh draft of sea breeze. His gaze returned to the delegates and spectators. He must measure his words carefully, being bold enough to incite the Southern Rights delegates into rebelling against their party and walking out of the convention, but not so inflammatory as to discredit his cause by inciting a riot among the packed rows of spectators.

He had first given this speech twelve years before to the Democratic Party Convention of 1848 in Baltimore. The primary question before the Democrats then as now was the disposition of slavery in the Western Territories. Yancey insisted the Democrats adopt a platform permitting slavery to enter all territories and be protected there by Federal authority.

Stephen Douglas and the Northern majority took a less extreme position, saying that slavery should only be allowed into those Territories where most settlers were Southern slaveholders but should not be forced into Territories settled predominantly by Northern Free Soilers.

Yancey was preparing again to tell the Southern delegates that because they could not trust Northern Democrats to protect their "right" to bring slaves into all Territories, they must dissolve the party. They must walk out of this convention and reconvene as a Southern Rights Party nominating its own candidate for President. His unspoken message was that if the South's pro-slavery candidate was not elected President, the Southern States would be justified in leaving the Union.

He remembered that when he had made this plea in 1848, most Unionist delegates, even those from his own state of Alabama, had shouted him down. Only one other delegate had followed him out of that convention. He had gone back home to Alabama to be ridiculed as a rabble-rousing Secessionist. He had responded by boldly reiterating his message: that if the North continued to block Southerners from taking their slaves into all the territories, then the South must look to its interests by leaving the Union and setting itself up as a separate Southern Republic.

He had repeated his message until events began to favor him. In the mid-1850s came "Bleeding Kansas," the armed conflict between Southern and Northern settlers over whether to allow slaves into Kansas. Then the rise of the "Black Republican" Party dedicated to prohibiting the spread of slavery over a single inch of the Territories. Then John Brown's Raid and Abolitionist hopes of instigating a slave uprising in the South. Then the Supreme Court's *Dred Scott Decision* that inflamed the North by declaring slaves to be lawful property in all states and territories. Northerners and Southerners insulted each other in the vilest terms and even to physically assault each other in the halls of Congress.

So many events had broken his way, he convinced himself Providence blessed his secessionist destiny. The most recent blessing was the selection of Charleston, the foremost Southern Rights city, to host this convention. The galleries were packed with "Fire Eating Secessionists" egged on by Charleston's radical newspapers. He thanked Providence for arranging events to bring him to the exact time and place where his words would have their maximum effect.

Next to patience, Yancey's greatest virtue was his power of persuasion, deriving from his broad life experience. He was born into a slave owning family in Georgia. After his father's passing, his mother had married a Yankee Abolitionist minister and moved to upstate New York. There Yancey became a strident nationalist, taking the position that attempts by states to defy Federal authority were treason. As an adult he had returned to the South to settle in Alabama, becoming a Southern Rights man dedicated to the principle that the South must either vindicate its "right" to bring slavery into the western territories or leave the Union.

Because he had embraced so many diametrically opposing ideas, he knew how to make almost any position sound convincing. When he used the phrase "States Rights" he meant:

"The Federal Government must protect the right of residents of the Southern States to bring our slaves into the Territories. The Federal Government must help us catch our runaway slaves, even if it means invading the homes of Yankees suspected of harboring them. The Federal Government must help us expand our slave territory by conquering Mexico, Central America, and Cuba. The Federal Government must enable us to reopen the African slave trade. *But in all other things **except** slavery the Federal Government must not intrude upon the right of the states to do as they please.*"

He denied being a Secessionist while saying that unless the Federal Government followed to the letter his view of States Rights, the Slave States would be "forced" to secede. He had learned how to make these contradictions sound reasonable to the delegates of the fifteen Southern Slave States he wanted to lead out of the convention and into a new nation.

He had husbanded all his strength for this momentous speech. He exhibited not a trace of nervousness, for he was accustomed to speaking before thousands and tens of thousands. He could sense the anticipation of the delegates and spectators in the galleries, anxious to hear "The Great Orator of the South."

He felt a surge of energy swell within him. He was as one with the Southern Rights men and women in his audience. He half-listened as Convention President Caleb Cushing called the afternoon session to order. In seconds he would be given the floor.

But then, instead of recognizing Yancey, Cushing brought up unannounced business.

"Honored Delegates, during the intermission I received a communication personally delivered by Senator Jefferson Davis. It is jointly signed by Senator Davis and Senator Douglas. As the communication is both brief and urgent, I will read it now."

Yancey's blood ran cold. He bolted out of his seat, standing up and waving the papers of his speech over his head.

"Mr. Chairman!" he roared, "it is out of order to read a communication when no motion is before the House! I am scheduled to take the floor and I respectfully demand it!"

In other circumstances Cushing would have deferred to Yancey, Cushing being one of those Northern Democrats who endorsed the South's views on slavery. But Senator Davis was a trusted friend. "Mr. Yancey," he implored, "please, I ask your patience. The letter is brief. It will require less than half a minute to read."

Alabama delegate John A. Winston, a Southern Unionist and long-time Yancey opponent, stood up, glaring at Yancey. "I motion that the letter be read!"

"I second!" shouted Mississippi delegate Joseph Davis, Jefferson Davis' nephew.

Yancey attempted to interrupt. "The proper way for the gentleman to communicate..."

Cushing bellowed to cut him off: "The Chair decides, upon the motion and its second, that as the communication refers strictly to the party platform, it will be read!" He began reading, his voice rising to a practiced crescendo: "A Letter of Compact between Senators Stephen A. Douglas of Illinois and Jefferson Davis of Mississippi."

Absolute quiet descended upon the convention floor and the galleries.

"Honorable Delegates of The Democracy, assembled in convention at Charleston: be it known that Stephen A. Douglas, a Senator representing the State of Illinois, and Jefferson Davis, a Senator representing the State of Mississippi, do solemnly pledge our united and unwavering support for the nominee chosen by our party. We are dedicated to

19

the unity of our party and committed to maintaining with our lives, our fortunes, and our sacred honor the perpetuity of this **Confederate Union of States.** We most sincerely implore the honored delegates to likewise dedicate themselves to the unity of our party and to the perpetuity of our **Confederate Union**. Signed Stephen Douglas and Jefferson Davis."

A tumult erupted from the floor and the galleries. Shouts of "Hear! Hear!" came from the Douglas men amid quieter murmurs of "Betrayal!" from a few of Yancey's Southern Rights delegates.

Cushing banged his gavel. "This meeting will come to order!"

The noise subsided to a murmur. "The Chair now recognizes the honorable William L. Yancey of Alabama. Mr. Yancey is allotted an hour and a half."

Yancey fought to regain his composure. *I expected this sort of nonsense from Douglas, but what has got into Davis? I planned for him to be the first President of our Southern Republic! What did Douglas promise to convince him to betray his future as well as ours!*

His breathing was shallow, and his heart raced. His mouth went bone dry. He feared his legs would buckle. "Gentlemen of the Convention..." he blushed as his voice squeaked. He coughed and had to start again. "Gentlemen of the Convention, my state has now to ask of this body the adoption of resolutions...."

As he remembered his carefully rehearsed lines, his voice became calmer. He remembered to manifest the proper demeanor of a reasonable man appearing to have been wronged. He regained his carefully crafted cadence. He claimed he was not a dis-unionist and did not know any. He alleged that dis-unionist sentiment sprang from the North because Northern Democrats had failed to do their duty to stamp out Abolitionist sentiment before it became strong in their states.

He said Northerners had no right to complain about slavery, "the highest order of civilization." He said Blacks were "destined to do the dirty work" that the white "master race" ordered them to do. He said that owning slaves elevated even the poorest of Whites to a life above menial labor. He said Stephen Douglas, the party's presumptive nominee, had betrayed the South's constitutional rights by failing to agree to uphold its unconditional right to take slaves into all territories.

Convention rules forbade the customary applause and cheering during his carefully timed pauses. He anticipated subdued whispers of "yes, that's right, go on" among a sea of nodding Southern Rights men. The last thing he expected was absolute silence and unmoving heads. The delegates and spectators seemed confused, as if they were trying to reconcile his words denigrating Stephen Douglas with the Letter of Compact that the revered Jefferson Davis had signed.

Damn that Stephen Douglas and his fool Jefferson Davis!

Yancey proceeded to the climax of his speech, telling the Northern Democrats that if they did not adopt his platform of unconditional support for expansion of slavery into the territories then the Southern Democrats would have no choice but to leave the party. He elevated the pitch of his voice to match its stirring conclusion:

"To my countrymen of the South I have a few words here to say. Be true to your constitutional duties and rights. Be true to your own sense of right. Accept of defeat here, if defeat is to attend the assertion of the right, in order that you may secure a permanent victory in whatever contest you carry a constitutional banner. Yield nothing of principle for mere party success—else you will die by the hands of your associates as surely as by the hand of your avowed enemy."

When he sat down there was a smattering of polite applause but not the raucous gallery-clearing tumult he anticipated.

Senator George Pugh of Ohio asked for the floor. Pugh was prepared to denounce Yancey as a dangerous agitator bent on destroying the Democratic Party and the nation. Now he recognized that the Douglas/Davis Compact cut the ground out from under Yancey. Instead of making an inflammatory speech attacking Yancey and his Southern Rights followers, he decided to offer reconciliation:

"Gentlemen of the Convention, I trust that the Compact between our two esteemed Senators Stephen Douglas of Illinois and Jefferson Davis of Mississippi will unite us in support of our party's nominee. Remember that if we do not elect the President, the platform will not matter. As for me, my trust in our party, its nominee, and its platform is sealed by the Compact of Douglas and Davis to maintain the unity of our party and the perpetuity of our ...Confederate... Union."

21

This time there were subdued sounds of approval from the floor and even from some Southern Rights spectators in the galleries. Chairman Cushing allowed the noise to die down then asked if there were any further business.

"We will vote for the Party Platform in Monday's morning session," he declared after a moment of silence. "We will vote for our party's nominee in the afternoon secession. This convention is adjourned until ten o'clock Monday!"

Yancey managed with difficulty to rise from his chair and make his way back to his hotel. Instead of accolades, most Southern Rights delegates did their best to ignore him. A few shook his hand limply. "Good speech, Bill," they said without enthusiasm, then left in a hurry before he could coral them.

It was Saturday evening. Yancey worked the hotel taverns and upstairs rooms, hectoring the intoxicated Southern Rights delegates to walk out of the convention with him if their slavery platform was voted down by the Northern majority on Monday.

"Three cheers for Yancey! Buy a drink for Bill!" shouted his most loyal friends. But most delegates paid no attention to his harangues. The few sober men who did said, "I don't know, Bill. Jefferson Davis has decided to unite the party behind Douglas. Maybe we had better take some time to think this through."

He walked briskly back to his room when the taverns closed their doors in the wee hours, passing delegates and spectators who stumbled along in the moonlight, a few howling like dogs. That Sunday morning, as the dawn brightened, the hotel rooms in Charleston buzzed with the snoring of delegates sleeping off their benders.

He awoke at ten but restrained himself until mid afternoon when he started making the rounds of knocking on the hung-over delegates' doors. Instead of telling Yancey to "go to hell" as they would have said to most any other delegate, the men with throbbing heads and dry mouths curtly nodded, hoping to get Yancey out of their hair as quickly as possible, without offending him. Sober delegates who had attended church that morning politely excused themselves when Yancey came knocking on their doors.

On Monday the fateful vote on the party's platform was taken. Yancey's slave plank was voted down, the more moderate position favored by Douglas delates prevailing by a margin of 185 to 118. Following the vote Yancey duly walked out of the convention, calling for the delegates of fifteen Southern Slave States to follow him. Two South Carolina delegates heeded him. So did two Georgia men and one each from Alabama and Mississippi. The rest stayed put, then proceeded, according to the Compact, to nominate their party's ticket of Stephen Douglas and Jefferson Davis.

Dan Elbert, one of Alabama's delegates uncertain about following Yancey, sat back down when he saw only six others leaving with Yancey. In that moment of profound silence, he involuntarily let out a loud, "Whew!" of relief that only they had gone.

That broke the tension. The hundreds of delegates who remained roared with laughter, then began whistling and cheering. Somebody up in the galleries unfurled a large American flag. As it caught the breeze and fluttered, the cheers of the delegates, Northern and Southern alike, rose to a crescendo that shook the building to its foundations.

"It looks like the Union flag of Washington, Jefferson, and 'Old Hickory' Jackson is safe for another generation," a delegate standing near a reporter was heard to say. The quote was the headline of the story of the convention's proceedings that most of the nation's newspapers reported on the following day.

Springfield Illinois, May 19, 1860

Abraham Lincoln addressed his Republican Party colleagues happily milling about in his Springfield law office: "Gentlemen, as the Democrats have done us no favors by dividing their party, let's make it our first order of business to do them no favors by dividing ours!"

"That's right, gentlemen," exclaimed Lincoln's boisterous friend and campaign manager David Davis. "Let there be no favors for Democrats! The last favor Old Abe did for a Democrat was to marry Mary Todd before Judge Douglas got around to it!"

Lincoln and his friends laughed with gusto. They knew how Mr. Lincoln and Senator Douglas had both courted Mary Todd as young bucks making their starts in Springfield. Although Mr. Lincoln was his party's candidate for chief magistrate of the nation, his authority at home was severely constrained. Stories of Mrs. Lincoln chasing her husband through the streets of Springfield with a rolling pin were the source of much mirth in town. There were many who supposed that Mr. Lincoln *had* done Douglas a huge favor by beating him to the punch in proposing marriage to the charming but temperamental firebrand.

Mr. Lincoln slapped his knee and looked over his shoulder in an exaggerated manner, pretending to make sure that no one else, and especially not his wife, was in earshot.

"Judge Douglas can't run as fast as Mrs. Lincoln, so I suppose that during this canvass I shall be able to keep a step or two ahead of him!"

Even the stern men among Lincoln's entourage laughed loudly. It was indeed a joyous celebration for Mr. Lincoln and his friends. The Republican Party's official delegation had come to town to notify him of his selection as the party's presidential nominee. It was a beautifully inspiring spring day outside as well, the sun tempered by passing rain showers washing the air breezing in through the open windows of Mr. Lincoln's upstairs office.

The celebration was diminished only by news that the Democrats had indeed failed to "do them the favor" of heeding Yancey's call to split the party into warring factions that could be beaten by the unified Republicans. In fact, the Compact between Stephen Douglas and Jefferson Davis had reinvigorated the Democrats, making them stronger than they'd been in years.

David Davis continued in his affable manner. "The story about Mr. Lincoln's courtship speaks to a remarkable situation. The two presidential contenders have made their careers together here in this little frontier town. They have become their respective parties' nominees because both parties know that to obtain an electoral majority they must carry Illinois. The election may be decided right here in the State of Illinois and very possibly by the voters of Sangamon County."

George Ashmun of Massachusetts, head of the Republican Party delegation, was strolling around the table loaded with ham, bread, and condiments. He waved a pickle between his fingers emphatically, as if it were a cigar.

"That's not to say that many counties aren't important," Ashmun emphasized. "I've been looking at the ones around New York City and Philadelphia. We'll need every vote we can get in those cities to carry the states of New York and Pennsylvania, which will also be necessary to make an electoral majority."

"That's what we were talking about on the way down here," Davis explained to Lincoln. "We're talking about running two campaigns, one that appeals to the interests of the East and the other appealing to Westerners. In the East we must talk about containing slavery and enacting protective tariffs, giving equal weight to each. Here in the West we'll talk about containing slavery, enacting the Homestead Act, and not a word about tariffs."

Davis addressed the entire group. "Another thing to remember is to 'Talk White.' Let the people know we are against the spread of slavery not just because it degrades the Negro but also because we want to protect the right of Whites to emigrate to the Territories and prosper there with free labor. When the Democrats call us 'Black Republicans' answer: 'We are the White Man's Party because we respect the rights of free labor. The Democrats are the Black Party because they want to spread Negro slavery to every part of this country.' So remember to talk Free Soil in the West. Talk tariffs in the East. Talk White Man's Party everywhere."

"While it is appropriate for us to campaign for the rights of White labor, let us not campaign *against* the Negro," Lincoln interjected. "I should not like for anybody in our party to campaign on the idea that the Negro, by the mere fact of his existence, is the cause of our national strife. Let's not join with those who seek to blame the Negro for problems of our own making."

The men nodded assent.

"Davis and I have been cyphering the electoral vote," said Ashmun. "We'll carry New England, Michigan, Wisconsin, Iowa, and Minnesota. Ohio will be close, but we'll have more Republicans campaigning there than Douglas men, so it's ours to lose. We'll carry Pennsylvania if we make our campaign clear on tariffs. To make sure of New York we'll have to keep the vote close in New York City and its environs. Mayor Wood believes the city's fortunes are tied up with the Southern cotton trade. To some degree he has a valid point. The New York banks do make most of their money lending to Southern planters. The shippers make most of theirs transporting Southern cotton to Europe. We'll have to convince New Yorkers that their fortunes are more tied to Northern industries, which we will protect with tariffs."

Ashmun crunched the last of his pickle then went on, barely pausing for breath. "Then there's New Jersey, which votes Democrat, but apportions its electoral vote. If we can make it close, we can pick up at least three of its seven electoral votes. And remember: we've got to direct our early efforts especially toward Ohio, Pennsylvania, and Indiana, which elect state offices in October. The early votes in October will certainly influence the national vote in November."

Lincoln's protégé Richard Yates, running as the Republican candidate for Governor of Illinois, had perched himself atop a table in between stacks of law books.

"We must use this election to stop the Slave Power," Yates said, frowning. "We've let them suborn the Supreme Court. We've let them take over in California and Oregon, after we brought them into the Union as Free States. Now we've let them set up shop in New Jersey and New York. While they're busy fighting us in the Free States they've shut us out from even campaigning in most Slave States. I'm beginning to wonder if *we* shouldn't be talking about leaving the Union!"

Lincoln looked up from the sheet of projected electoral vote tallies.

"Have patience, Dick. I am certain we will carry the entire Northeast except for a couple of New Jersey's electors. We have it in our power to carry the entire Northwest, and we will do so with a strong campaign. If we accomplish that, we will prevail in the Electoral College. Let's devote our energies to accomplishing what we can accomplish and not worry about what is beyond our reach."

Elmer Ellsworth, another of Lincoln's fiery young Republican friends who was renowned as the organizer of the Republican parade around soldiers known as the Chicago Militia, was agitated by the discussion. He'd been munching a ham sandwich until he heard Yates say the Republicans were prevented from campaigning in the Slave States. "Why **aren't** our men allowed to campaign in the South?" he asked sharply.

"The Slave States allege that our campaign to restrict slavery encourages slave revolts. Incitement of slaves is a violation of their Slave Codes," Ashmun replied, as he returned yet again from the table holding a piece of sliced ham.

Ellsworth jumped off the table. "Balderdash! The Bill of Rights protects the free speech of every candidate!"

"The First Amendment prevents the Federal Government from restricting the people's right to express their opinions," explained Ashmun. "The Slave States will argue that it doesn't prevent the states from restricting it, at least where anything that might be construed as criticism of slavery is concerned. Most Slave States won't allow our candidates on their ballots, not that we'd have any chance of winning their electoral votes even if they did. Like Mr. Lincoln says, there's no point in getting incited by it."

Ellsworth pointed his finger. "If they won't even allow us on the ballot, then it's not a legitimate election," he said decisively. "Our next job will be to amend the Constitution with a new Bill of Rights to make the Slave States respect it. Until then, if any Republican candidates want to campaign in those states, my men will be pleased to accompany them. We will force the Slave States to give them a fair hearing, even if it has to be at the point of our bayonets!"

A couple of the delegates laughed nervously, while the more thoughtful men kept silent. Sending a Northern militia company into the Slave States would ignite a civil war as soon as the company crossed the Ohio River.

Lincoln put his hand on Ellsworth's shoulder. "Let's not talk like that. If we make our case persuasively here in the North, we will win the electoral votes we need. Let us devote our energies to making our case to the people of these states who *will* listen to us."

Ellsworth wasn't satisfied. He stopped chewing his sandwich and looked sternly at Mr. Lincoln. "If the time ever comes when you need my militia to protect your right to be heard in *every* part of this Union, rest assured we will be ready."

4

Washington City, June 23, 1860

Stephen Douglas held court with his entourage at his residence in Washington City. Jefferson Davis wasn't there, having no taste for Douglas' liquor and cigar extravaganzas, nor for that matter any personal affinity for Douglas. But Douglas and his friends were having the time of their lives. The session of Congress had adjourned. With official business finished they were relaxing in boisterous good company, joyously contemplating the prospect of the rambunctious Stephen Douglas replacing timid James "Old Buck" Buchanan in the White House and thereby restarting the nation on its glorious Manifest Destiny, sidetracked so long by pointless debates over slavery.

Douglas raised his glass of whiskey through the smoke-filled air yet again.

"Now, gentlemen, let's begin our campaign to save the country! Confederate Union, United Expansion!"

He was proud of that catchphrase. He had coined it to let the voters know it meant more Slave States for the South and more Free States for the North. That, he hoped, would rally moderate voters to his party's standard, defeating the militant anti-slavery Republicans in the North and the die-hard remnant of Southern Fire Eaters clinging to Yancey.

Douglas snorted a whiskey belch, spit a piece of cigar wrapper on the floor.

"I'm counting on Davis and Breckinridge to hold the Slave States. They'll keep Yancey's band from picking off Mississippi, Alabama, and South Carolina. Aleck Stephens will hold the line for us in Georgia. Sam Houston will hold Texas. We'll also send Davis to New York, Boston, and Portland. He'll speak to the workingmen who don't want the slaves set free to take their jobs. Caleb Cushing and Horatio Seymour will accompany him. We'll make the Republicans fight and fight hard, in their own bordello! Who knows, but we might even take New York."

"We will carry it!" shouted his friends, raising their glasses.

"The Ohio Valley will be *our* battleground!" Douglas exclaimed, barely pausing for breath. "We need all the counties between the Ohio River and the Old National Road, and I mean all of them! We need the immigrant precincts in Chicago and South Bend! Let's get what we can out of the Dutch and Irish in Milwaukee. We might as well make Wisconsin as close as we can."

Douglas gestured to Illinois Congressman John 'Blackjack' Logan.

"Blackjack will be working Illinois from Alton east to the Wabash and south to the Ohio. While he's doing that, I'll be receiving audiences in Chicago. I'm advised not to break with tradition and take to the stump, but if I have to make a wee journey or two beyond Chicago then so be it!"

The men laughed at the image of Douglas campaigning like a whirlwind across Illinois and Indiana while pretending to honor the tradition of never leaving his hotel residence in Chicago.

Douglas turned next to Tennessee Senator Andrew Johnson who was relishing his shots of whiskey in a rare night of indulgence away from his strict wife. Douglas winked at Johnson.

"Andy's going to stump for us in New Jersey, then work his way through Pennsylvania and Ohio then into Illinois and Indiana. His message will be: 'Men of any party who advocate destroying the Union and repudiating the Constitution are preaching treason!' "

Johnson's whiskey-veined nose swelled red and his eyes shown bright. "Damn right!" he thundered. "Those fire-eating sons a bitches in the Plantation Aristocracy must be taught that secession is treason. So do the damn Abolitionists who talk disunion from the North. As for me, I don't care which bank of the Ohio a Secessionist stands on. A traitor is a traitor in any direction!"

The men shouted their approval.

Douglas took another draft of whiskey and made himself heard over the uproar. "That's the message, Andy! We must make clear that anyone who desires to divide this country is a traitor no matter what direction he comes from!" He held up the bottle. "Care for a refill?"

Johnson snorted. "Twist my arm!"

"The way the rain's beating on the roof we might have to stay here all night," said Caleb Cushing as Douglas poured the whiskey. "That would be a hell of a shame, wouldn't it, Andy?"

The room echoed again with laughter.

"Boys, I heard some troubling news the other day," Douglas said in mock seriousness. "A young inventor came by my office seeking funding for what he called a 'telegraph exchange.' Said he wants to build an exchange with telegraph lines connecting every home with every other one. That's going to put a crimp on some of us when our wives start asking us to call home every hour, especially you, Andy!"

"The world's changing, isn't it?" commented 'Blackjack' Logan when the laughter subsided. "I don't think the day will be long in coming before each of us *will* have a telegraph in our home. If we can run a telegraph to Europe we can run one anywhere and everywhere. Won't be long before every nook and cranny of the country, and maybe the entire world, is connected. Our job is to keep the country united today, so we'll be able to profit from progress tomorrow."

"Yes, here's to progress! To the future! To Confederate Union, United Expansion!" Douglas shouted, the force of his breath parting the curtains of cigar smoke. He saw his life's ambition to enter the White House nearing fulfillment. He would end the country's internal squabbles over slavery and then direct the national energies outward, towards the acquisition of Latin America to the South and the British Possessions to the North. A new

31

nation, coextensive with North America, would rise, its people for the first time truly united and assuming their rightful place as the greatest power of the Earth.

The others didn't know precisely how the plan for "United Expansion" would be carried forth. Nor did Douglas, despite his confident bluster.

Douglas' entourage did know that victory in the election would be very good for them. They would receive their due allotment of Cabinet positions and leadership of Congressional committees. Their party, its Northern and Southern factions united, would finally rule the national roost as one big happy family. Those noisy, trouble-making Republicans would be sent packing off to obscurity, never again to disturb the nation's peace.

Douglas knew what they were thinking. He was proud of them and confident they would convince voters to elect the party to the White House and Congress. He congratulated himself for doing what a party leader was supposed to do, which was to unify the party and provide it with a sensible campaign theme. "Confederate Union, United Expansion" appealed to sensible people in the North and South who wanted to keep the country together. It had already quashed the fire eating Secessionists at Charleston. He anticipated it would teach the militant Abolitionists that their schemes to disrupt the Union were equally futile.

Each day he felt more confident. His party was united, forcing the crazy Republicans to campaign from divided camps. Some talked like fanatical Abolitionists determined to destroy slavery by making war against the South. Some bent over backward the other way trying to accommodate the South. Some talked about leaving the Union in a huff. Some talked about protecting business with tariffs. Some talked about free trade. The voters were bound to be confused by all those conflicting ideas. His instinct told him they were unlikely to trust a party of such disparate views to govern them.

While Douglas was lost in thought, the room suddenly grew quiet, and he heard the rain pound down. The sudden silence unnerved him.

"Well, my friends, it looks like we're going to be here all night, so we might as well make the most of it. Let's have another round."

He puffed heartily on his cigar and poured himself and his friends another round of whiskey. That was enough to get Andy Johnson going with another one of his off-color stories about the backwoods of Tennessee. The silence was replaced by guffaws as Andy unwound his story, the one having to do with the farmer's daughter and the pumpkin patch.

5

Lancaster, Ohio, August 18, 1860

John Sherman   William T. "Cump" Sherman

William Tecumseh "Cump" Sherman was in "high feather" during his visit to the family home in Lancaster, Ohio. It was the return leg of his trip to Washington and New York to purchase equipment for the Louisiana Military Academy. As the recently appointed Superintendent of the Academy, Cump was getting along famously with Louisiana's governing plantation aristocracy who appreciated his military efficiency and personal character.

Sherman chuckled to himself as he remembered how his Louisiana friends had asked him to become a citizen of the state so he could pursue a political career there. He had made it clear that he was a military man who had no use for politics or politicians. During his two days here in Lancaster he had made it abundantly clear to his brother, Congressman John Sherman, how much he detested the politicians of both parties for what they had done to the country with their squabbling.

The Sherman brothers were having their morning coffee on the veranda, the air humid but pleasantly cool with fog lingering between the hedges.

"Cump, I want to tell you in confidence that my party is alarmed about the election," said John. "We have our doubts about being able to beat Douglas and Davis. If those two get to the White House I'm afraid the nation can't remain united under one flag."

"Why the hell not?" Cump answered, with hot breath from his coffee steaming in the foggy morning air.

John grimaced. "Because we can't even *talk* to their party. Every time we confront them about halting the expansion of slavery it turns into a shouting match. Soon it's going to be fisticuffs. A family that can't talk to each other can't live together under the same roof."

"And *who* do you blame for *that*?" Cump answered with disdain. "You politicians have got things into a hell of a fig, and you may get them out as best you can! Thanks to you this country is sleeping on a volcano." He turned his head away to show he did not want to continue the topic. What would *he* do if his brother threw in with those Republicans who wanted to bust up the country?

His brother wouldn't drop the discussion. "Cump, another thing is that Douglas looks bad. He's drinking himself into an early grave. I'm wondering if he gets elected if he'll even live out his term. If he is elected and passes away, Jefferson Davis will become the next President. I have no brief against Davis personally, but this country can't stand another Southern Rights President. The Free States will be provoked into leaving the Union."

Cump put down his coffee. "They're both campaigning on a Union platform. Davis is shouting for the Union as loudly as Douglas. 'United expansion' and all that. What's wrong with that?"

"It's the 'expansion' part that worries me," John replied. "Southerners want to expand their slave territory. How can they do that other than annexing Mexico? Then we'll get a vigorous enforcement of the *Dred Scott Decision* that opens the entire country to slavery. Then they'll bring in the West as Slave States and put a ring around us. They'll recognize a Slave State constitution in Kansas. They'll divide California and open a new Slave State on the Pacific. They'll use *Dred Scott* to come chasing after the free Negroes living here in Ohio. They'll turn this country into the greatest slave empire since Julius Caesar's!"

Cump shrugged. "None of the slave owners I know in Louisiana talk that way. As far as I can tell, they just want to be left alone to work their Niggers and grow their cotton and rice. Why don't you people on this side of the Ohio learn to mind your own damn business?"

John swatted a fly away from his coffee. "You wait and see how they talk after Douglas and Davis put the idea of turning this whole continent into a slave empire in their heads."

"It sounds like you've given up on the election."

"No, I haven't given up," John said sternly. "I'm going to fight like hell to save this country and keep at least part of it as Free Soil. But it is a normal thing in politics to have your ducks in a row in case you lose an election."

"So, your Republicans are going to take your 'ducks' home if you lose, are you?" replied Cump sarcastically. "You're going to go out of the Union and into your own country? Have you heard Mr. Lincoln say anything about it?"

"No," answered John. "I haven't heard him say anything other than that we must trust the people to vindicate our position at the ballot box. It's Chase, Chandler, Sumner, and Fremont, plus the usual Abolitionists who are talking about leaving the Union. They're trying to bring moderate Republicans into their camp."

Cump thrust his chin out defiantly. "Well, they'll have to get past Stephen Douglas, if you're right about him becoming the next President. I don't think he'll allow the Free States to leave the Union. I don't think he would mind hanging some of those Abolitionists, and he'll do it if they keep talking treason."

John guffawed so hard he barely kept from spewing his coffee. "You've got to be joking! He's leading a party committed to State Sovereignty. How can he deny the right of the North to secede after all their hurrahing for the right of the South to go out of the Union any time it pleases?"

"A few of the Southern Rights fanatics may believe that nonsense," Cump countered. "But Douglas doesn't. He's a patriot. If your Republicans and Abolitionists start making noises about leaving the Union, he'll stop you. So will us old Army men. We're sworn to uphold the Constitution and we'll carry forth our duty to maintain the integrity of this Union. You better believe we will. If you participate in any plot to break the Union, you will be a party to treason. Think about it before you do anything you'll later regret."

John replied carefully, hoping to avoid inciting his brother. "It's none of my business, Brother, but I'm guessing you've decided to cast your ballot for the Democrats. I wish you'd think about your decision thoroughly because the vote here looks close." Both Shermans were citizens of Ohio and voted here.

"If the Democrats had split their party in Charleston, I'd vote Republican just to keep the election from being decided in Congress if the electoral vote got split three or four ways," retorted Cump. "Now I think the Democrats have the right idea to keep the country united. The Republicans sound confused and desperate. The patriotic vote is for Douglas and Davis."

John shook his head. "You've been down in Louisiana too long. The heat must have affected your mind." He went back inside leaving Cump to finish his coffee alone.

Cump frowned. What if his brother was right about the Republicans wanting to take the Free States out of the Union? Would the Slave States care? Hotheads like Yancey certainly wouldn't. They'd say, "Good Riddance!" But Cump thought the Douglas Democrats would stand foursquare behind their party's pledge to maintain the Union.

Perhaps the Abolitionists would be able to take New England out of the Union. But they'd have a real fight on their hands in the other states with more significant business and family ties to the Slave States. Many voters in these states were Democrats who lapped up their party's anti-Negro, pro-slavery propaganda as eagerly as any Southern slaveholder. They'd prefer to stay in a Union with the Slave States than go off into another country with Abolitionists. There would be partisan strife, maybe civil war all over Ohio, Indiana, and Illinois if the Republicans tried to bust up the country.

Cump didn't think Douglas would tolerate that for a moment. He'd do what any Union-loving President would do, which would be to march the Regular Army, reinforced by militia from the loyal states, through the disaffected states in a show of federal authority. George Washington had raised a federal army to put down the Whiskey Rebellion in 1789. Andrew Jackson had threatened it against South Carolina's Nullifiers in 1833. Cump wondered if he'd find himself called up to lead a division of Louisiana Militia in a war to subjugate Ohio's Abolitionist rebels. Would he find himself at war with his own family here in Lancaster?

He decided not to continue thinking along these unhappy lines. Perhaps the country would settle down and get back to business after the votes were counted. He stood up and followed his brother back inside the house. He called to him, "Let's take a walk around town. Who knows when I'll be able to get back up here."

6

Springfield, Illinois, September 15, 1860

Stephen Douglas clenched his teeth as he sat down at the back of the podium and waited for Abraham Lincoln to rise and take his turn. Douglas wished to be anywhere other than here with Lincoln, the only man he had never bested in debate.

Lincoln's performance in the debates of the 1858 Illinois Senate campaign had propelled him to national prominence, though Democrats retained enough seats in the State Legislature to send Douglas back to the Senate. Now the two candidates from the frontier town of Springfield, Illinois met once again to debate for the highest elective office on Earth.

Many who came to this great debate wished it were held in one of the large cities like New York, Cincinnati, or Chicago. Big-city accommodations would have better sheltered the throngs of spectators and catered to the expense accounts of newspaper editors. As it was, most slept in the town's rented rooms at extortionate rates if they could afford them, or out on the fairgrounds if they couldn't.

Springfield was selected to preserve the custom of presidential candidates campaigning from their homes, though it hadn't been Douglas' physical home in more than a decade. After being elected to the Senate in 1852 he had relocated his residences to

Chicago and Washington City. Springfield most certainly was his political home as judge, Congressman, Senator, and now his party's presidential nominee.

Perhaps it was more than coincidence that Lincoln and Douglas both hailed from this little town. Springfield, by its location along the great divide between North and South, represented the views of the national electorate. Born of the North, the South, and the West, it had matured both candidates' political careers by presenting them with the views of all sectional constituencies, especially on slavery. And Springfield's voters were important in their own right. Whoever won Springfield would probably win the State of Illinois. Whoever won the State of Illinois would become the next President.

Douglas looked at the enormous crowd, estimating it at well over a hundred thousand. At the front were over five hundred reporters taking shorthand notes. Behind them people stood shoulder to shoulder for acres. Further still were those who had ridden in on wagons drawn by horses and oxen. Making themselves heard would strain the well-practiced voices of both candidates.

This great crowd made Douglas immensely proud of the American Republic. A moist trace of sentimental tear fell from his eyes as he thought of the majesty of popular democracy. The people were here to respectfully listen to him and Mr. Lincoln, then use their sober judgment as free citizens to decide who would be their next President. They had so far respected the candidates' wishes to make their voices heard. There had been a few spontaneous cheers from excited spectators on some salient points made by the candidates, and some laughter, especially at Mr. Lincoln's witty lines. But no disruptive shouting or catcalls.

As thrilling as this debate was, Douglas would have avoided it if he could have done so without hurting his chances in the election. He had calculated that refusing Lincoln's challenge would make him appear weak and evasive.

He grimaced again as he read the paper Lincoln had handed him as they exchanged places on the podium. The Interrogatories portion of the debate had started. According to the agreed upon rules, Lincoln provided four questions for Douglas to answer. Then Douglas would reciprocate with four questions for Lincoln. Each candidate had already given an opening statement. After the Interrogatories, each would make closing statements.

Lincoln gave his opening statement as Douglas expected. He spoke his often-repeated position that he had no quarrel with slavery where it already existed in the Southern States. If elected President, he would govern with a fair regard to the South's interests in enforcing the laws of protecting its slave property as every other president since Washington had done. He would only oppose the expansion of slavery into the national territories yet to become states.

Douglas responded by trying to tie Lincoln into the Abolitionist Camp of Frederick Douglass, John Brown, William Lloyd Garrison, Owen Lovejoy, Wendell Phillips, and Charles Sumner, who spoke out for the immediate liberation of slaves. Douglas tried, as always, to paint this group as a militant cabal of radical agitators hell-bent on wrecking the Union by constantly insulting Southerners in the vilest terms and doing all they could to incite their slaves to rise up against them.

Douglas detested these Abolitionists even more than the Southern Fire Eaters.

Southerners are prideful and stubborn on slavery because it is the foundation of their society. I might excuse some of them for saying silly things in its defense. But I cannot excuse the Yankee Abolitionists for inflaming and inciting Southerners, hoping to drive them from the Union. Yancey would never have come so close to breaking up our party and endangering the Union if the damn Abolitionists hadn't paid for John Brown's lunatics to go down there and try to whip up a slave rebellion. If Lincoln is elected, they'll keep on trying until they wreck the Union.

He sought to undermine Lincoln by appealing to the people's anti-Negro sentiments. He knew that the Whites whose votes he needed to carry Illinois and Indiana wanted Negroes to remain in bondage to prevent them coming north to compete with white laborers. Douglas claimed that Lincoln not only wanted to free the Negroes but to grant them social equality with Whites. "Lincoln joins with those who want to free the slaves and then marry them off to your daughters!"

Douglas felt he had to use this line of attack to discredit Lincoln, but he did not relish it. Although Lincoln was older by several years, Douglas was his senior in politics, having been nationally prominent long before Lincoln was known beyond Illinois. He saw Lincoln as something of a precocious little brother who annoyed his older brother by acting as if he was smarter, but who was nevertheless loved and admired.

41

Douglas looked at Lincoln in that fraternal way even while cursing his anti-slavery politics. He therefore read Lincoln's questions with a mixture of admiration and annoyance. He knew from past debates that Lincoln's questions could be devastating in cracking open the inconsistencies between the shifting positions Douglas had taken in his attempt to reconcile the Slave State South with the Free State North. In the Senate race of 1858 Lincoln had knocked down Douglas' Popular Sovereignty platform like an outhouse in a tornado.

Douglas read the questions as Lincoln spoke them:

"Question 1: Has there been any agreement between Senator Douglas and Senator Jefferson Davis to acquire territory from Mexico, Cuba, Central America, or any other country for the purpose of bringing said territories into the United States as Slave States?

"Question 2: If there has been such an agreement does it involve war as an action to force said foreign territories to enter the Union as Slave States without the consent of the people who now inhabit them?

"Question 3: Have Senators Douglas and Davis agreed to direct their efforts toward definitively closing to slavery any territories now owned by the United States or that may be acquired in the future?

"Question 4: If Senators Douglas and Davis have entered into such an agreement to close said territories to slavery how does Senator Douglas reconcile this closure to the Supreme Court's ruling in the *Dred Scott Decision?*"

As he had feared, Lincoln wasted no time raising the most vulnerable points. He wondered if someone had communicated the unwritten terms of his compact with Davis to Lincoln. Douglas hadn't discussed these terms with anybody other than Davis, but perhaps Davis had spoken to others who were loose-lipped. Or perhaps Lincoln had simply deduced that such terms were necessary to persuade Davis and his Southern followers to unite with Douglas.

Douglas knew from experience how to debate Lincoln. He knew better than to try to refute Lincoln by answering his questions directly. Above all else, he did not want Northern voters to know that his compact with Davis was based on the military conquest of Mexico. Many Northerners predisposed to voting for him might decide otherwise if they became aware that he had already committed himself to a war to spread slavery over foreign soil. But Douglas' sense of integrity, however malleable, forbade him from pretending the discussion had never taken place. He decided his best response would be to answer each question partially but not completely.

He took the podium and reread each question before answering it.

"First Question: I am asked if there has been any agreement between myself and Senator Jefferson Davis to acquire territory from Mexico, Cuba, Central America, or any other country for the purpose of bringing such territory into the United States as Slave States.

"Senator Davis and I *have* discussed the question of acquiring new territories for the United States. We are agreed that the national policy will be that the settlers of any present or future territory lying south of the Missouri Compromise Line of 36-30, shall have slavery if the inhabitants so choose it. Settlers north of 36-30 shall remain free to prohibit it.

That reaffirms the Missouri Compromise Line without mentioning Mexico.

"Second Question: I am asked if there has been any agreement between myself and Senator Davis that war will be used as a method of forcing foreign territories into the Union as Slave States without the consent of the people who now inhabit them.

"My answer is that the United States is a civilized nation that desires the acquisition of territory by honorable purchase.

That is how we desire to acquire territory. But if the avenue of peaceful acquisition is closed to us, then war may become necessary. I am counting on France to give us the excuse to acquire Mexico by military intervention. After we have the country in our possession, Southerners can decide how much of it they desire to settle. That portion of Mexico will be admitted to the Confederate Union. We'll find a few inhabitants we'll persuade or pay to "consent" to it.

"Third Question: I am asked if I and Senator Davis have agreed to work to definitively close any territories that may be acquired in the future to slavery.

"The answer is 'Yes' as I explained in my answer to the first interrogatory. Senator Davis and I are agreed that the national policy shall be not to extend slavery north of 36-30.

43

"Fourth Question: I am asked to reconcile the agreement between myself and Senator Davis to close the territories north of 36-30 to the Supreme Court's ruling in the Dred Scott Decision declaring all Territories open to slavery.

"The reconciliation is this: The Supreme Court has ruled that slave owners *may* take their slave property into all our national territories. But the Court's decision does not *compel* them to emigrate to free territories. We anticipate that slave owners will not want to bring their slaves into the territories north of 36-30 because they will be provided with sufficient territories south of that line. We will thereby respect the Supreme Court's decision that although slaves *may* be taken into all the territories, their owners will *choose* not to take them into those territories north of 36-30."

Wasn't that a clever answer!

A few scattered cries of "That's fair!" showed that Douglas' answers were effective.

"And now, it is my turn to present interrogatories to Mr. Lincoln," said Douglas. He reached into his coat pocket, pulled the written copies of the questions, handing one to Lincoln sitting behind him, then reading from his copy:

"First Question: Does Mr. Lincoln believe that any political party whose appeal is limited to a specific section of the country can successfully govern the entire country?

"Second Question: Does Mr. Lincoln believe the ultimate status of the Negro is to be freedom in all states and territories of the Union?"

"Third Question: If Mr. Lincoln answers in the affirmative, does he believe that the Negro must ultimately be made a citizen in every state with equality of political, civil, and social rights, including the right to vote, to serve on juries, and to intermarry with the White race?

"Fourth Question: Does Mr. Lincoln believe the Free States, acting through the Federal Government as their agent, have the authority to compel any state to change the status of its Negroes in regard to ending slavery or the granting of civil rights to free Negroes?"

The candidates switched places again as Lincoln took the podium to respond. Lincoln read from the paper that Douglas had given him.

"I am asked first if I believe that any political party whose appeal is limited to a specific section of the country will be able to successfully govern the entire country. Let me say that it is exceedingly desirable that parties should find adherents in all parts of the country. President Washington eloquently warned of the danger that political parties pose to the Union especially if organized along sectional lines.

"Neither I nor anyone I am aware of in my party has any loyalty superior to the nation. Judge Douglas should ask himself whether this is true of his own party! He should ask himself if there is not a faction of his party that devotes itself to promoting the interests of a particular section ahead of the interests of the nation as a whole, even to the point of threatening disunion. I refer to the faction of Judge Douglas' party that declares that its peculiar interest of slavery must not only be protected where it exists but must be allowed to expand to its entire satisfaction; otherwise, it will go out of the Union and form itself into a separate nation. Does Judge Douglas himself not advocate for this faction of his party against the national interest?"

"Yes, he certainly does!" answered a spectator near the front of the crowd.

"Then it seems to me that Judge Douglas has the duty to eliminate the sectional interest in his own party before he complains about the sectional interests of other parties!"

"That he does!" shouted the same voice.

"I will answer now the questions concerning the ultimate fate of the Negro Race in America," continued Lincoln. "I cannot help but comment that of the four questions allotted, Douglas is concerned in three of them with the status of Negroes. Does he believe that three-fourths of our national issues concern Negroes, even though they are but one-seventh of our population? How can it be that a man who tells us on every occasion that the Negro is an inferior being of no account in the political life of our nation should so concern himself with the Negro's fate? But you must be your own judge of Douglas' motives in making the Negro the central issue of his campaign. I will limit myself to answering the questions as he has asked them:

"Douglas asks if I believe the ultimate state of the Negro is to be freedom in all states and territories of the Union. The direct answer is 'Yes.' I do believe the ultimate status of the Negro will be freedom in all the states and territories. I expect that attitudes

45

will change slowly over the course of many generations until freedom is perceived to be the natural condition of all men, as is so clearly stated in our Declaration of Independence.

"In the next question I am asked if, having answered in the affirmative that the Negro is ultimately destined for freedom, whether I believe that the Negro is also ultimately destined to become a citizen of every state with complete equality of political, civil, and social rights, including the right to vote, to serve on juries, and marry Whites."

Lincoln chuckled. "My friends, I have had the honor of debating Judge Douglas on many occasions. I don't recall a single occasion when he did not ask me this question of Negroes being permitted to marry Whites. His purpose is to insinuate that because I am opposed to the extension of slavery, that I must also desire that Negroes and Whites should marry. He knows that I have already answered several times previously that just because I do not want a Negro woman for a slave, it does not mean that I must have her for a wife. I can also just leave her alone. But Douglas must always insist on maintaining laws that forbid marriage between Whites and Negroes. He must fear that the men who follow him desire Negro women for wives and must therefore depend upon the force of law to prevent it!"

The Republicans in the crowd, and even a few Democrats, roared with laughter.

"In regard to the question of social equality, I will leave it to each person to choose to associate with whomever he pleases. Those who don't prefer the company of Negroes do not have to associate with them. Now, as to the other elements of Judge Douglas' question, as to whether Negroes should be allowed to vote, to serve on juries, and so forth, that is a question for each State to decide, as they already do. Judge Douglas himself points out that most of the New England States allow their Negroes to vote. In New York Negroes may vote provided they own at least $250 in property. They do not vote in other states. Each state regulates the Negro as it chooses. There is no controversy on this point.

"The defenders of slavery attempt to justify the institution by saying they do not believe the Negro capable by intellect or disposition to enjoy any degree of freedom. I will not for the moment quibble as to whether the Negro is entitled to full equality of political and civil rights. But I do believe the Negro is entitled to certain God-given rights. He is entitled to eat with his own mouth the bread that the labor of his own hands produces!"

Shouts of, "Yes, that is just!"

"In the final question I am asked if I believe the Free States, acting through their agent of the Federal Government, may coerce or compel any state to change the status of its Negros, against the wishes of its people. The answer is that the Constitution makes clear, according to every reasonable interpretation, that the Federal Government may not interfere with the condition of Negro servitude in any state. Each state is to be the sole and absolute authority over the status of its Negroes, deciding whether the Negroes will be slave or free, and if free whether they will be granted civil rights on a basis of partial or full equality with Whites."

Douglas and Lincoln again exchanged places so that Douglas could deliver his closing statement. Douglas addressed the crowd:

"I have known Mr. Lincoln for more than twenty years. I do not believe that he would ever purposefully do anything to endanger the integrity of this Confederate Union. However, there are many who *would* use Mr. Lincoln as their sword to tear apart this great confederation by provoking a war between the North and the South.

"All one has to do is read the public statements of Fred Douglass, Wendell Phillips, Owen Lovejoy, and Bill Garrison to understand that they want to eliminate slavery immediately by any means, including making war upon our white brothers in the South. No one can deny that John Brown had this intent when he attempted to incite the slaves into bloody revolt against their masters. No one can deny that other villains of like intent would take encouragement from Mr. Lincoln's election. With encouragement they would spring to action. The South would with reason fear that such attacks were imminent and would take the necessary remedies to protect itself. No matter what Mr. Lincoln might or might not decide to do personally, his election would threaten the existence of this Confederate Union.

"Whereas Mr. Lincoln's election can only threaten the Confederate Union, the Compact between myself and Senator Davis is designed specifically to save it, not only in the present time, but for all time to come. The Free States and the Slave States will each have their opportunities to expand within our common country. Confederate Union, United Expansion!"

Douglas sat down. Lincoln rose to make his closing statement:

"Judge Douglas professes to hold a most curious view of me. He professes to believe that should the people choose to elect me as their Chief Executive, that I would sit idle in

47

the White House while the devils that Douglas conjures up from the depths of his fertile imagination set out to make war on the South. He wants you to believe that perhaps I would even encourage such a war."

A voice from the crowd: "You would not do it!"

"Judge Douglas should remind himself that the war between slave owners and Free Soil men began in Kansas as a proximate result of his revoking the original Missouri Compromise, replacing it with his so-called doctrine of Popular Sovereignty allowing slavery to go wherever the slave owners please. Now he tells us that Popular Sovereignty was a grievous error. He promises to replace this grievous error with his compact with Jefferson Davis, the secret terms known only to himself and Davis. Ask yourselves why he has proclaimed this Great Compact to be the salvation of the Union, yet he does not desire that the public should know its substance?

"I have made no secret compacts with anyone. My views have always been open and well known to the public. I have never had to recant them. My actions as President will not be mysterious. They will be no different from those of any previous President from the time of the Founders. We know from their speeches and writings that presidents Washington, Adams, Jefferson, and Madison wished for an end to slavery. Yet none used the office of President directly or indirectly to affect the status of a single slave. Even if I did desire to use the office of President to disturb the institution of slavery, the Congress, which will in all probability retain its present majority, would not allow it. I will have neither the inclination nor the authority to interfere with the status of a single slave in any state.

"Now, it is true that as a matter of personal preference I do not favor slavery. I do not like bickering about whether this one man should be the other's slave because the one man is presumed to be darker or less intelligent than the other. My faith is the Founders' faith that all men are created equal. That is the true founding principle of our country. However, we must govern according to the laws and customs as they are today and trust that they will become more enlightened in later generations. I will govern according to the laws and customs of my time, not those of a future time when I do sincerely hope that all men shall be free.

"But neither will I bargain away our future as a free nation by allowing slavery to spread to territories where it does not now exist. I will keep the faith with those of the

48

present generation who own slaves, while also keeping faith with future generations by governing on the principle of our Founders that slavery should one day disappear from this land. When it does disappear, it will be done by the will of the people in the states where the institution now resides.

"I can not know the secret details of the Douglas/Davis Compact, which Judge Douglas takes so much pain to conceal from the public. You cannot know them. My intentions are honest, unchanging, and open for all to see. I trust the people to give them a fair hearing."

The debate was finished. Douglas and Lincoln clasped each other in a genuine display of respect and affection.

"Be well, my friend," said Douglas.

"And you," answered Lincoln. "Let us both remember that one of us will have to govern the country after the election. Let us take care to say nothing now that will complicate the task."

Douglas smiled and tapped Lincoln on the back, walking off the podium with confidence. He had to admit that Lincoln's closing statement had bested his. On the other hand, he felt that he had bested Lincoln with the Interrogatories. At this moment perhaps the debate would be seen as a tie. But tomorrow his campaign would be bringing Andrew Johnson, John Bell, and Blackjack Logan into town. They would put forth the idea that Douglas had won the debate. Most likely they would convince the press that this was so, and the press would convince most of the voters. He smiled to himself. His Democrats were much the Republicans' masters at molding public opinion.

If we can keep this up for six more weeks, we will save the Union.

New York City, September 22, 1860

George McClellan   Elmer Ellsworth

George McClellan clasped both hands on Elmer Ellsworth's shoulders. "Magnificent demonstration, simply magnificent!"

Ellsworth saluted crisply. "Thank you, sir! I am truly honored by your approbation. I'm so glad you enjoyed our little drill!"

McClellan and Ellsworth had come to Battery Park in New York City to cheer their parties, Ellsworth as a Republican and McClellan as a Democrat. Both parties were hosting gigantic rallies. The Republican speakers were allotted the early afternoon. New York Senator William Seward was the keynote speaker, followed by the demonstration by Ellsworth's militia company. For the evening events, the Democrats had former New York Governor Horatio Seymour followed by Jefferson Davis, a speaker popular in New York City for his view that Southern Rights must be maintained from within the Union.

Both parties spent heavily on their respective rallies because both thought they could carry the state. Upstate New York would vote massively Republican, while New York City and neighboring Brooklyn, with their polyglot workingman's population and strong business ties to the South, were Democratic strongholds.

The resurgence of the Democrats with Douglas and Davis heading their ticket had turned it into a real contest. That Republicans had to spend so much time and money here indicated their campaign was not going as well as expected. New York's thirty-five electoral votes should have been safely in their column.

The Republicans were wooing the voters with a clambake and beer. Democrats offered roast beef sandwiches and whiskey. McClellan wandered back and forth between the two camps on this beautiful sunny afternoon, partaking of clams and roasted beef in a nonpartisan spirit. He had thoroughly enjoyed the Republicans' rousing patriotic show, especially the drill by Ellsworth's militia.

"I am so glad to see old friends from Chicago," McClellan told Ellsworth. "You and your militia have given the city something else to be proud of."

"Thank you again, sir," Ellsworth replied. "May I ask what brings you to New York? Will you be speaking on behalf of the Democrats this evening?"

"Oh, no," McClellan answered. "I wear many hats, but never the hat of a politician! I came to New York on railroad business. When I learned of these rallies, I extended my stay. I want to hear the views of both parties, though I am partial to the Democrats. Jefferson Davis was like a father to me as Secretary of War. As you know, he entrusted me with several missions of significance to the nation."

"I've read your articles about the Crimean War," said Ellsworth. "And I know of your work in surveying harbors in the Caribbean. If Mr. Lincoln is elected I am hoping that perhaps he will select me for some of these missions."

McClellan smiled. "Don't worry about that, my friend. I promise you will have nothing to lose no matter who sits in the White House. I will recommend you to Douglas and Davis if they're elected. You are a worthy military ambassador for our nation regardless of your party affiliation."

Ellsworth gave a perfect salute. "I am truly honored beyond words to count you as my friend. I hope we may have a long association in the common cause of serving our country. If you'll please excuse me, I must lead my men to dinner as guests of honor of Senator Seward. They've had a long day."

McClellan watched Ellsworth leave. Ellsworth's company was equipped with money raised by Republican Party men. The Republicans sponsored many such outfits, Ellsworth's the most professional. The more amateurish groups were called "Wide Awakes". Their men didn't carry arms but manifested paramilitary discipline by wearing approximately the same "uniform" and marching in a tolerable order. They were here by the thousands too, singing Republican campaign songs and easily recognizable by their thick black capes and the torches they would light as evening fell.

Although the Wide Awakes had given no indication of wanting to make trouble for the Democrats, there was something about them that made McClellan uneasy. For one thing they were mostly young men in their twenties, sharp and alert. The ones McClellan had bantered with were articulate in explaining why they backed the Republicans.

The Democrats had their paramilitary groups called the United Invincibles here too, but they were more interested in drinking free liquor than listening to speeches. Most were rough-and-tumble workingmen who could not articulate any reasons for their Democrat affiliation other than that the Democrats "talked the language" of uneducated city men who labored with their hands.

The differences between the two groups alarmed McClellan. If most young men in the North, especially the smart and disciplined ones, hitched their wagons to the Republicans then the Democrats' days would be numbered. McClellan had gleaned from conversations that these young Wide Awakes also had a sense of nationality subtly different from his own.

Whereas McClellan saw himself as an American with warm ties of friendship to the North and South, the Wide Awakes saw themselves exclusively as Free State men. They talked as if the Slave States were another country, mired in backwardness and even barbarism.

A few told McClellan they supported Republicans because they thought enslaved Negroes should be liberated, but most seemed to want to steer clear of all Southerners regardless of their color. One said they wanted a free country of their own, untainted by slaves or slave masters. McClellan wondered whether they would still consider the United States to be their country if Douglas and Davis prevailed. Or would they feel they were aliens in their own land?

McClellan also knew young men in the Slave States who wanted nothing to do with the Free State North. The young men in both sections were growing apart. Only the old-timers who had come of age in an era of shared national triumphs from the War of 1812 to the Mexican War seemed to want the country to stay united.

McClellan hoped the Democrats could hold out against the rising sectionalist tide long enough for Douglas and Davis to win the election. Although he had not been told the secret terms of the Davis/Douglas Compact, he surmised that they intended to be aggressive in acquiring new territories, even to the point of going to war.

McClellan was no warmonger, though he did believe that wars to acquire new territories in Mexico and Canada might be necessary to consummate U.S. hegemony over the whole of North America and to solidify the country's internal unity. He would look forward to personal glory commanding soldiers in the field. His current job as railroad president left much to be desired. He was fatigued with worrying about the minutia of loading freight and passenger cars to capacity every day.

McClellan heard cheering on the Democrats' side of the park, He presumed it heralded the arrival of Horatio Seymour and Jefferson Davis, so he started meandering through the crowd in that direction. He wanted to say "hello" to Davis and invite him to dinner before he left town if his schedule permitted. He had a sudden curiosity to know more about the secret details of the Douglas / Davis Compact, specifically if there might be opportunity for him to lead troops back into Mexico.

8

Boston, October 17, 1860

William Lloyd Garrison   Frederick Douglass

William Lloyd Garrison's face seethed with agitation as he looked at Frederick Douglass.

"I had expected, and I dare say I had hoped, that this election would set the Free States and Slave States to war," confessed Garrison. "That is the only way I can see of setting your people free. But the Republicans have become as timid as Quakers at a shindig!"

Frederick Douglass was also angry, but his face brightened as he tried to conjure up Garrison's unlikely image of Quakers.

"Yes, no doubt that both parties mean to sacrifice the Negro, same as always. They are busy kissing each other's arses while once again conspiring together to sell the Negro down the river."

Garrison crumpled up the newspaper article he'd been reading aloud and tossed it into the fireplace. It was a transcribed speech by Republican Senator William Seward of New York given two days before.

Seward was the anti-slavery stalwart who had coined the phrase "irrepressible conflict" to describe what he believed to be the impending collision between the Free States and Slave States. But in this most recent speech he called for "accommodation between the Free States and the Capital States." Garrison and Douglass looked at each other in disgust when Garrison read the "Capital States" euphemism implying that enslaved human beings were just another ledger of capital investment like livestock!

"I truly am sorry," offered Garrison. "I expected better of my friends. Alas, Mr. Lincoln is silent while Seward has withdrawn his friendship from us entirely. They were chastised by their losses in the state elections, so now they're trimming their sails. Their willingness to sacrifice the slaves in order to placate their masters sickens me."

"You've got nothing to be sorry about," Douglass assured him. "As long as there are hearts like yours, so brave and true, the Negro will not lose hope. When we first met, you advocated almost alone for my race's freedom. Now millions are with us. We will never give up. We will raise our children to carry on the fight, and we *will* carry it on generation by generation until every person born in America is a free and equal citizen."

"God bless your patience," answered Garrison. "Only He knows when your race's shackles will be broken. But that day will come. It will come sooner than we think."

Douglass felt a burden of anxiety lift from his shoulders. He had come here hoping to renew an old friendship now estranged. He had not been sure that Garrison, a stubborn and egotistical newspaper publisher, would reciprocate.

"I am so pleased to be back in the embrace of your friendship," said Douglass, who had offered to make amends by consolidating his Abolitionist newspaper *The North Star* with Garrison's *The Liberator*. "We should never have grown apart. We are fighting for a cause larger than ourselves."

"Perhaps I'm becoming more patient in my old age," replied Garrison. "I always saw the Constitution's guarantees of slavery in the Southern States as a Pact with the Devil that must be broken by getting our Free States into a new country of our own. After seeing how Southern Secessionists are so anxious to break up the Union, to perpetuate slavery, I've become more inclined toward your view that dividing the nation would perpetuate slavery in an independent South. But whatever differences we have on that question, we *must* agree that it is futile to waste our efforts going off into separate camps and squabbling among ourselves. The Democrats have united their party around a Union with slavery. We must unite our party around a Union that is free."

"So true, my friend," confirmed Douglass. "Let's salute the new united voice of all Abolitionists: *The North Star Liberator!*"

"We're going to have our work cut out for us in stiffening the Republicans' backbones," replied Garrison. "After that drubbing, they took from the united Democrats in the state elections in Indiana, Ohio, and Pennsylvania, they're running away from their anti-slavery creed like scared rabbits."

Garrison sighed. "Every time we get to the verge of accomplishing something definite in the way of limiting slavery, the slave masters threaten to leave the Union. Then the Republicans start trying to outdo them in support of slavery. What hypocrites!"

"Their backsliding only encourages slave masters to make more extreme demands," agreed Douglass. "Did you see Stephen Douglas' last speech from Chicago? He said America's Manifest Destiny to expand westward to the Pacific Ocean is complete. He says now we must expand to the north and south. That means Mexico and the Canadas. The Slavers will conquer Mexico. Then they'll get us into a war with Great Britain over the Canadas."

Garrison threw down the draft of an article he'd been writing.

"What position should we take now? I'm not disposed toward endorsing Republicans, not after their cowardly retreat in Seward's speech. But if we endorse Gerrit Smith's Abolition Party we will draw the Republicans' enmity. We may cost them the election by dividing the Abolitionist vote. If we've learned anything, it's not to divide our forces and weaken our chances later."

Frederick Douglass walked over to the window. He saw the sun setting over the tree line. Garrison had a portrait of George Washington on his wall next to the window. Douglass recalled the story he'd read about how Washington had contemplated a carving of the sun cut into his chair at Constitution Hall, wondering if it was rising or setting on America. He reflected on how Washington had persevered to bring the new nation to life, through bitter defeats, bitter cold at Valley Forge, political intrigues in the government, and incipient rebellion in his army.

Douglass could likewise persevere in liberating the slaves. He was more patient than Garrison, even though born a slave. He had experienced the mind-numbing work, the poverty of inadequate food and clothing, and the brutal discipline. He had seen Negroes beaten and even shot down like dogs for refusing to obey their overseers.

Douglass possessed wisdom allowing him to see the fallacy of advocating the end of slavery through violence and civil war. He therefore sought to moderate Garrison's fiery editorials in the combined *North Star Liberator*, channeling them toward liberating the slaves gradually but constitutionally. He had an inspiration. He turned from the picture of Washington and toward Garrison.

"Let's not waste our efforts tying ourselves to either party. Why don't we instead take a lesson from the slave owners? What do they do every time they think an election isn't going their way?"

"They call a convention where they all get together and start shouting about leaving the Union," Garrison answered. "Then when the North backs down they go back to pretending to be loyal Americans."

"Exactly," said Douglass. "They call a Slave State convention where they huff and puff until the Free States back down. They did that in Nashville in 1850. They wanted to do it in Charleston until Douglas fooled them with who-knows-what kind of promises. Why don't *we* call a Free State Convention? Let's do some huffing and puffing on our own. Let's see if we can't get our Republican friends to take us as seriously as they take the slave masters."

Garrison parted his thinning hair. "A Free State Convention? That isn't at all a bad idea. We *should* call a convention to put freedom first and parties second." He paced over to stare outside the window next to Douglass. "We'd better do it sooner rather than later. A couple weeks after the election. If the Republicans lose, their voters will be angry. They'll want a forum to blow off steam. It will be our chance to make our voice heard loud and clear. I wonder where we should have it --- Boston, New York, Philadelphia, or Washington City?"

Douglass thought a moment. "We shouldn't call a Free State convention in Washington City, where slaves are held. There are too many anti-slavery agitators in New York and Philadelphia who might disrupt the convention. Having it in Boston would make it look like a New England affair. Maybe Chicago? We have enough friends there to fill a convention hall."

"Not Chicago," Garrison replied. "It's too remote. And it's associated with the Republican Convention that nominated Lincoln. If he loses, it will reflect badly on us to be seen following in his footsteps. If he wins it will look like we're riding his coattails."

"What about Cleveland, then?" Douglass suggested. "It's a strong Abolitionist city. It has good railroad connections to all the Free States. Let's set the convention date the week before the next session of Congress convenes. The Free State Congressmen will have time to attend and then make their way to Washington City for the start of Congress."

Garrison paused to think. "I can't think of any reason why it shouldn't be in Cleveland. I was there last summer, and you're right about the good hotels and rail connections. The 27th of November might be a good date to start it. That's three weeks after the election, easy to remember, a week before the next session of Congress. If the Republicans win, I don't expect they'll bother to attend. If they lose, they'll be there to vent steam. That's when they'll need us to help them get back on their feet. Are you agreed, then, that we should call our Free State Convention in Cleveland on the 27th of November?"

Douglass liked the proposal. "I think Cleveland will do."

"Excellent!" replied Garrison. "Well, our dinner should be about ready. Let's discuss this convention while we eat, then we'll come back here and set the type. We can proof it in the morning and go to press tomorrow."

The more Garrison thought about the Free State Convention, the more enthusiastic he became. If the Republicans won the election, the Free State Convention would be there to remind them that Abolitionists were a vital part of their constituency. If they lost, the Convention could become the foundation for a stronger Abolitionist Party. Perhaps it might even become the foundation of a new United States, a nation true to the principle that all men are created equal ---- The United States of **Free** America.

9

Cleveland, Ohio, November 25, 1860

Why would anybody want to live in Cleveland? Abraham Lincoln wondered about that as he kicked the snow off his shoes and brushed the flakes from his coat before entering the Weddell House hotel. The temperature was well below freezing as a stinging wind blew fresh snow squalls in off Lake Erie, which seemed perfectly placed to convert winter air into wet snow. When he'd left Springfield three days ago, the temperatures were twenty degrees above freezing with sunshine.

"Welcome to Cleveland, Mr. Lincoln!" said the doorman as he entered the hotel. "I think you'll find the Weddell House warm and comfortable, and I hope conducive to your business." Lincoln walked to the registration desk, still scuffing his shoes to knock off the last splotches of snow. The doorman directed the porter to take his bags. "Too bad about the election," he said. "I'm sure you'll do better in '64."

Lincoln brightened. "Thank you, and thanks to all in Ohio for coming through for us this time around." When he finished signing the registration he added, "You are right that we have every reason to be optimistic. The way our Republican constituencies are growing, we will surely prevail sooner rather than later."

A fashionably dressed young fellow standing near the door recognized him. "We surely will, Mr. Lincoln," the man said enthusiastically. "We'll elect you President next time, you can count on that! You just wait until the people discover what Douglas and Davis are up to!"

Lincoln shook the man's hand. "You just wait until Douglas and Davis discover what *each other* are up to!"

The man guffawed. "Yes, indeed, what a pair we've elected! They're liable to kill each other before you run again. By the way, I'm Ignatius Donnelly, Lieutenant Governor of our great new State of Minnesota. I do hope we'll see you on the ticket again in '64. We need to put an end to this slavery nonsense before it poisons the whole country."

"We need to put an end to this Republican Party nonsense before it poisons the whole country," interjected a man in rumpled clothing next to him.

"Don't pay him no never mind," said Donnelly. "That's Jim Goodhue, publisher of *The Minnesota Pioneer* in St. Paul. It's the most profane Douglas scandal sheet in the entire Northwest!"

Lincoln shook Goodhue's hand. "I reckon you've had more than your fill of my speeches already, if you've been printing my debates with Judge Douglas."

"Yes, sir!' replied Goodhue. "I must confess you were most eloquent in defending your positions, though I remain convinced that Douglas got the better of it with his 'Confederate Union, United Expansion!' line."

"Thank you for reporting these debates to your readers," said Mr. Lincoln with obvious sincerity. "I'm glad you came here to give your readers an account of these proceedings, even if you don't agree with them. Our democracy could not long endure without editors of the free press such as you."

Donnelly snorted. "It's crazy editors like him who make the best argument *against* a free press!"

"And its politicians like you who make the best argument against popular democracy!' retorted Goodhue as he slapped Donnelly good-naturedly on the back.

Lincoln smiled. "Since you men came all the way here from Minnesota, I suppose we'll have to put on a good show to justify your travel vouchers!"

Lincoln was pleased that Donnelly did not seem angry with him for failing by the narrowest of margins to carry the Republican Party into the White House. The Republicans might well be inclined to give him another chance in '64. Parties didn't usually give losing candidates another chance, but who could say? It *had* been a very close election. On the other hand, he was disturbed that a Douglas Democrat newspaper editor was thriving in Minnesota. A state that far north should have been settled by anti-slavery New Englanders. If a Democratic newspaper editor had a readership large enough to make the paper profitable, then perhaps the Republicans were not as strong as Lincoln thought.

"Meet us around the bar after you get settled," Goodhue proposed, "and we'll rustle you up a drink or two."

"Thank you very much, gentlemen, but I've been travelling for three days straight, while being called upon to speechify at every station! I must have my beauty rest." The men laughed at Lincoln's self-depreciating humor about his appearance. Lincoln felt better. If Republican politicians and Democratic newspapermen were still drinking together, then there was a fair chance all would yet be well.

As soon as he reached the registration desk the clerk handed him a sheaf of messages. "A lot of people have been asking for you."

He was surprised so many were already here. He had arrived two days early, intending to have a good rest today followed by relaxed socializing tomorrow before getting down to business on Tuesday. "How many are you expecting?"

"Over five hundred have booked. Hotel's full. Manager says over eight hundred are expected, including those who booked at the hotels across the street."

"Eight hundred? Well I'll be jiggered! I was wondering if anybody other than me would be here."

"The Free State Convention is big news in Ohio," the clerk said cheerfully. "Must be in other states too."

For a moment Lincoln thought about peeping around the corner to see if anyone he knew was in the common are, where a modest buzz of conversation was in progress. But he was exhausted from the three-day train ride and the disruption of his sleep last night by an unscheduled stop when the locomotive boiler lost pressure. If he became involved in

61

political gossip it would go on until late in the evening. Better to rest now, awaken refreshed, and be primed to talk long into the night. He told the clerk, "If anybody asks for me, please tell them I'll be down for dinner. Will you send someone up to wake me at five?"

As he followed the porter up to his room he reflected on the conversations about the election. He had narrowly lost the two states whose votes were most closely contested --- Illinois by only 5,400 votes out of 340,000 and Indiana by 2,200 out of 270,000. Illinois was as much Stephen Douglas' home state as it was his, but even so, losing it hurt. The people in Sangamon County who knew him best had voted a majority for Douglas.

He wondered again if he should have broken with tradition and campaigned more actively. Douglas had done it, and though the Republicans had mocked him as an uncouth demagogue, he had garnered the votes needed to put Illinois and Indiana in his column, thereby giving him the electoral vote majority. Douglas had bested him by 63% to 37% in the national popular vote, a resounding win, but not unexpected considering the Republicans had not been allowed to campaign south of the Ohio and Potomac rivers.

 The deciding factor had been the Douglas/Davis Compact. It had done its job of persuading the majority that the Union could best be maintained by continuing to trust its fortunes to a united Democratic party. Many Northern voters had decided not to force a break with the South by electing a Republican President. Many would surely have switched their vote to Mr. Lincoln if the Democrats had listened to Yancey in Charleston and turned against each other.

He anticipated events he believed would work in the Republicans' favor. Douglas was elected, now he would have to govern. His strategy of trying to be all things to all people was bound to catch up with him. Lincoln chuckled to himself as he imagined Douglas taking fire from front and rear by Yancey's rump of States Rights Democrats as well as the Republican Free State voters.

Douglas might very well destroy his popularity trying to thread his way between these factions, as he'd come so close to doing with Popular Sovereignty in the 1850s. If Douglas started marching and countermarching around in circles, he would surely make a fool of himself, enabling the Republicans to be elected in a shoo-in in the next elections.

Perhaps Providence would yet transform Mr. Lincoln's defeat in this election into a blessing in disguise. Sometimes losing an election was best for the candidate and the party, although it rarely seemed so at the time of the loss. He cyphered that the next election would have a more Republican constituency in Illinois and Indiana. These states were settled first from the south by Kentuckians and Virginians moving north across the Ohio River. These people followed their fathers' tradition of voting Democratic. Only later, after the completion of the Erie Canal, had enough New Englanders and foreign-born Europeans, primarily Germans, began arriving in the northern counties along the Great Lakes to make the states competitive for Republicans.

Ohio, being a few years ahead of Indiana and Illinois in its settlement, had already acquired a larger Republican constituency. Though it had given the Republicans a scare in the early state election of October, vigorous late campaigning had swung its presidential electors into the Republican column in the national election. And beyond the Mississippi there was fertile ground for new Republican-voting Free States --- Dakota, Colorado, Nevada, Kansas, Nebraska, and Minnesota. His weather-beaten countenance brightened again when he thought he might yet live to see a Republican President, even if someone other than him.

When they reached his third-floor room, the porter opened the door and set down the bags. He showed Lincoln the room and asked him to call if he required anything else. The porter smiled and said, "Thank, you, sir" when Lincoln tipped him. Lincoln reflected that most porters were Negroes like this fellow. Few white laborers wanted to "demean" themselves by carrying another man's bags. Negroes did the work cheerfully, earning tips in fine hotels like this one exceeding the wages paid to Whites who labored in farms and factories.

He hoped that Negroes, at least here in the North, would remain free and unmolested until Republicans could make a comeback. Southern slave owners could be counted on to use the election of Douglas and Davis to their advantage. The *Dred Scott Decision,* combined with a vigorous enforcement of the Fugitive Slave Law, would encourage them to scour the Free States for runaway Negroes, perhaps even kidnapping free Negroes and selling them back into slavery.

The slavers would find plenty of accomplices among the rabid anti-Negro men of the North. He was embarrassed by the Democratic majority in the Illinois Legislature who'd recently voted to arrest idle Negroes and hire them out as indentured servants, a practice to all intents and purposes equivalent to slavery. Plenty of Whites were glad to turn any Negro who annoyed them over to slave catchers and collect their bounty.

He therefore felt his party must walk a tightrope across this Free State Convention. They couldn't say anything to make their party appear radical and sectional. After all, the New England Federalists had destroyed their party in 1814 by threatening secession at the infamous Hartford Convention. Indeed, if Yancey and his Southern Fire Eaters had prevailed in Charleston, the Democrats would have destroyed their party and Mr. Lincoln would have won.

On the other hand, Republicans had to remain vigilant to guard against the Democrats infecting the entire nation with pro-slavery sentiment. The Democrats had the White House and a majority on the Supreme Court. They dominated the Senate 40 to 26. Republicans held a narrow majority of 125 to 114 in the House. Their House majority plus the recent innovation in Senate rules known as "The Filibuster" should enable them to quash any pro-slavery legislation the Democrats tried to ram through Congress.

However, we must take nothing for granted. Douglas and Davis will have no qualms about working around our Republicans in Congress, even if they must bend the Constitution to its breaking point. They will be supported by the Southern Democratic majority on the Supreme Court and by the governors of fifteen Slave States marching in lockstep. They have many friends in the Free States --- including the Democratic governors and legislatures of California, Oregon, Illinois, and Indiana. We, in turn, must make common cause with the moderate Union-loving men of the Upper South who tolerate slavery, but are indifferent to its expansion. We must be noisy in keeping our cause alive, but not obnoxious in threating to leave the Union.

He sat down on his bed and read through the sheaf of messages he picked up at the desk. There was a note from his closest colleagues in Illinois, including Richard Yates, Senator Lyman Trumbull, Congressmen Owen Lovejoy and Elihu Washburne, and David Davis, informing him they would be arriving together tomorrow. Other prominent Republican friends including Senator Ben Wade from Ohio and Michigan's Zach Chandler had already arrived and asked him to call on them. Abolitionists Gerrit Smith, William Garrison, and Frederick Douglass wanted to meet with him. The last message was from the great Pathfinder John Fremont, the Republican Party's presidential nominee in the prior election of 1856, who was coming in from California.

Again, he fought the temptation to greet his colleagues now. The fatigue in his body told him he was no longer the young man who could ride on horseback all day on the Illinois circuit court, arrive at a country tavern at sundown, talk politics into the wee hours, and then arise the next day for court.

Before taking his rest, he pulled open the curtain and looked at the view outside. Through the swirling snow he looked across the broad street and took in the panorama of the city. *So this is why people come to Cleveland!* The Cuyahoga River opened into a large harbor. A boiler factory and a rolling mill stood next to a lumber yard. This was one of those places on the Great Lakes where iron, lumber, coal, and commerce met; where Capital and Labor prospered together. People of all walks of life flocked to these places. Cleveland, like Chicago, was destined to grow into a large city. It would be the task of this convention to make certain that it, and the other great cities of the North, remained Free State cities, with staunch Republican anti-slavery constituencies.

Our best hope of ending slavery is for the Southern slave owners to observe the prosperity of our free laborers in the North. They will come to understand that slavery has no future and will abolish it on their own. That will not happen in this century, but perhaps in the next. In the meantime, we in the Free States must not allow our lamp of freedom to be extinguished by those who seek to educate the people to the idea that slavery is the natural and permanent state of the dark-skinned peoples who live among us.

He removed his coat and stretched comfortably on the bed. He smiled to himself as he thought how far up in life he had come, staying in a top shelf hotel where each guest had not only a bed all to himself but also a room. Just a few years ago he'd ridden the circuit through dusty prairie towns in Illinois, sharing flea-infested beds with strangers in packed rooms. But how he had loved those days! Talking law and politics with other itinerant lawyers in those little inns until way past midnight. These big-city hotels had their luxuries, but they would never compare with those boisterous good times he had had with his associates in those crowded little taverns out on the prairies.

He fell asleep reminiscing about political talk around the fireplace in the late hours of a winters' night back in the mid 1850s when he had been a prairie lawyer instead of a candidate for national office. During his dreams he vividly recalled those happy fire-lit conversations, though perhaps the voices filtering through his sleep were those of other arriving delegates talking in the hall.

Cass County, Michigan December 11, 1860

Notwithstanding the snowy landscape and the howling wind outside, Eddie Bates felt warm to the depths of his soul.

"We're going to be free, Emma, really and truly free!" he shouted to his common law wife in the kitchen, as he held up his copy of *The North Star Liberator*

"You're gettin' mighty excited for this early in the morning," Emma answered back. "What do Mr. Fred Douglass and Mr. William Garrison say that's got you so stirred up?"

"It's not Mr. Douglass and Mr. Garrison this time. It's Mr. 'Honest Abe' Lincoln and Mr. John 'Pathfinder' Fremont promising Negroes will be free. They's talking about the ones up here in the Free States, not the ones down South."

"That sounds more like it," said Emma, bringing in the wood-carved plates and forks. "Sounds like they's promising to free the Negroes what's already free and leave the ones that's slaves alone. Don't seem like reason enough to get exited to me."

"They's more to it than that," said Eddie, ladling field peas onto his plate. "Fremont says from here on out any Negro makes it across the Ohio River and settles down without getting caught right away is a free man. That means *us*. We don't have to worry about the slave catchers no mo'. That's something, don't you think?"

"Don't take it for granted just yet," Emma replied. "White folks *have* been known to make promises they didn't intend to keep. What, exactly, did Mr. Lincoln and Mr. Fremont say?"

Eddie and Emma lived in the limbo common to the residents of the Negro Settlements straddling the border of Indiana and Michigan from South Bend to Battle Creek and Kalamazoo. Most of the Negroes had lived free for years, but few had legal title to their freedom. Eddie's family had run away from a Maryland plantation in 1833 when Eddie was 9. Emma had walked out of her owners' house near Wilmington in the Slave State of Delaware when the master passed away in 1850. A few hours later she was in free Pennsylvania, disappearing anonymously into Philadelphia's Negro district.

Southern slave catchers were entitled by the Fugitive Slave Act to apprehend Eddie, Emma, and any other Negroes who could not show proof of their title to freedom. The Fugitive Slave Act not only authorized Southern slave catchers to prowl the North looking for "runaway" Negroes, but required all citizens including law enforcement officials to assist the slave catchers in returning Negroes to slavery.

So far the Whites in the Abolitionist communities of southwest Michigan and adjoining St. Joseph County, Indiana had defied the Fugitive Slave Act by protecting their Negro neighbors. Marauding slave catchers were surrounded by mobs of enraged citizens and told they would be killed if they ever returned. The threats were effective. Slave catchers hadn't been seen in Cass County, Michigan or St. Joseph County, Indiana since the early 1850s.

Even so, Eddie never risked travelling beyond the little area encompassing South Bend and Kalamazoo. Not all Northern Whites were Abolitionists. Many, even in these parts, would cheerfully turn him over to slave catchers because they despised free Negroes and needed the bounty money. Even the protection of his Abolitionist neighbors in Cass County couldn't be counted on as an absolute guarantee of his safety.

In past years former President Franklin Pierce had threatened to send the national army into the North to subdue the Abolitionists and capture the Negroes they protected. Pierce had backed down, but Eddie fretted that President Stephen Douglas with Jefferson Davis at his side would do it in a heartbeat. He had imagined the arrival of a Federal Army commanded by militant Southerners surrounding Cass County then going house-to-house to sweep every Negro up into captivity.

Eddie was especially at risk because his family's escape had been recorded by their owners as a property loss. He had felt cold fear in his belly when a neighbor had once shown him his name in the classified section of a Detroit paper identifying him as a runaway slave known to be at large in Michigan.

Emma was more secure because her former owners had long since passed away. Their heirs had never bothered to retrieve an inherited runaway house servant. But she would never be entirely safe because she had no proof of manumission. Her title of ownership was still somewhere in the Delaware probate courts. Furthermore, slave catchers merely had to claim they were her former owners. There weren't very many whose consciences would be troubled by giving false testimony claiming that any Negro they happened to run across had once belonged to them. Without proof of manumission she was at any slave catcher's mercy.

For months after the election, Eddie was so terrified of Douglas and Davis that he had not slept well. He had kept waking up in nightmares of being returned to slavery. He had talked to Emma about crossing the unguarded border into the British Possessions in the Canadas, even though he had been warned that British subjects were no fonder of Negroes than were most American Whites. He was tortured for months wondering whether to take himself and Emma to an unwelcoming foreign land or to stay put and risk being returned to slavery.

Emma finally persuaded him they should stay. "We shouldn't let the election of Stephen Douglas and Jefferson Davis cause us to run us away from our homes and our friends. This is as much our country as theirs. If all the free colored folks in the North run off to Canada, who's going to be left to speak out for our people down South?" Eddie reluctantly agreed, but still woke up many mornings in a cold sweat, having a premonition of being returned to slavery.

Then *The North Star Liberator*'s glorious report of the Cleveland Convention dispelled his fear. Eddie had read the paper many times already and still felt warm relief welling up inside him. Although he often spoke in the semi-literate vernacular he grew up with as a slave, he had been educated in the Quaker schoolhouses after his family's escape to Michigan. He frequently read aloud with a theatrical persona honed from church readings and community plays. In his practiced baritone voice he read the newspaper report to Emma:

Mr. Lincoln's address to the Free State Convention in Cleveland, Ohio:

If we could first know where we are, and whither we are tending, we could then better judge what to do, and how to do it. Let us first consider where we began our journey. Let us go back to that great Age of Liberty in the Time of our Founders and examine where they were and whither they were tending.

Of the founding of our nation John Adams said:

"I always consider the settlement of America with reverence and wonder, as the opening of a grand scene, and design in Providence, for the illumination of the ignorant and the emancipation of the slavish part of Mankind all over the earth."

George Washington concurred:

"The citizens of America, as sole lords and proprietors of a vast tract of continent, are the actors on a most conspicuous theater which seems to be peculiarly designated by Providence for the display of human greatness and felicity."

And Thomas Jefferson told us most eloquently:

"We hold these truths to be self-evident, that all men are created equal and are endowed by their Creator with certain inalienable rights, that among these are life, liberty, and the pursuit of happiness."

Our Founders left us no doubt as to whither they tended. From the North and South alike, they had a common vision of the United States spreading Liberty across this continent by our government, and around the world by our example. By their actions they demonstrated that slavery should be neither an enduring part of our government nor of our example.

They constantly expressed the hope that slavery would gradually be extinguished by the advancing state of civilization. Mr. Jefferson himself authored that great Ordinance of 1787 that forbade the introduction of slavery into our Northwest. George Washington urged the Virginia Legislature to abolish slavery, and fell but one vote short of garnering the majority necessary to abolish it.

Until about thirty years ago this sentiment was expressed almost as often in the South as it was in the North. Indeed our distinguished delegate John Fremont is a Southern man, born and raised in Savannah and Charleston. It was not uncommon for Southern men of his generation to be tutored by their elder statesmen to advocate for the constraint and eventual demise of slavery, which they knew to be consistent with the wishes of our Founders, of whom at least half were Southerners.

Thus, it was until recently that we knew with certainty that we were tending in the direction of perfecting this Republic by constraining slavery and securing in the public mind the understanding that it was in the process of ultimate extinction.

Now let us examine whither our President-elect is tending. Said he during our recent debates:

"I do not believe that the signers of the Declaration of Independence had any reference to Negroes or to the Chinese or Coolies, the Indians, the Japanese, or any other inferior and degraded race, when they spoke of the equality of men.

"I don't care whether slavery is voted up or voted down; whoever wants slavery has a right to have it; upon principle of equality it should be allowed to go everywhere; there is no inconsistency between free and slave institutions; a negro slave being property, stands on an equal footing with other property, and the owner may carry them into United States territory the same as he does any other property, including dry goods and liquors."

Does it appear that President-elect Douglas is tending in the same direction that John Adams was tending when he said that Providence had designed America for the "emancipation of the slavish part of Mankind all over the earth?"

In his constant referring to Negroes as property with no more rights than dry goods or liquors, does it seem that he is tending in the same direction that Thomas Jefferson was tending when he said that all men are created equal and are endowed by their Creator with the right to life, liberty, and the pursuit of happiness?

And now the President-elect speaks of his ambition to expand our American Republic to include the whole of North America and its surrounding islands, caring not whether slavery should be "found" already existing in these lands:

"The time may come, indeed has now come, when our interests would be advanced by the acquisition of Cuba. When we get Cuba we must take it as we

71

find it, leaving the people to decide the question of slavery for themselves, without interference on the part of the federal government, or of any State of this Union. So, when it becomes necessary to acquire any portion of Mexico or Canada, we must take them as we find them."

And here, in regard to Mexico, he gives voice to the great misrepresentation of his ambition, for he will "find" Mexico to be a free country, having abolished slavery from its soil more than forty years ago. He does not intend to leave Mexico as he "finds" it. He intends to graft slavery onto Mexico, like a cancer, after having unleashed the Southern Militiamen to conquer the country, knowing full well that they are bringing their slaves in train.

Does it appear that the President-elect is tending in the same direction as our founding President Washington who perceived our free Republic to be "designated by Providence for the display of human greatness and felicity?" Or is Douglas tending towards the opposite direction of enslaving a free country, to graft upon it an institution designed for the display of human oppression and melancholy?

According to the President-elect, not only the Negro but also the "Chinese, the Japanese, or any other inferior and degraded race" may be enslaved. Presumably he is speaking of the Mexicans too, for are they not as dark as the Chinese or Japanese? And then, when the Negro and all these other "inferior and degraded" races are doomed, and damned, and forgotten, to everlasting bondage, is the white man quite certain that the tyrant demon will not turn upon him too?

That, my friends, is the perilous direction whither Mr. Douglas is tending. It is the direction precisely opposite of the great Design of Liberty that our Founders planned for this nation.

"What do you think about that?" asked Eddie.

"Mr. Lincoln does have a way with words, he surely does," said Emma when Eddie finished and took a long pause to catch his breath. She was inspired by Mr. Lincoln's words but didn't want to excite Eddie with false hopes. "Remember, dear, we've heard those kinds of words before," she cautioned. "Whenever white folks get to fighting over the Negroes you know what they do. They sell us Negroes down the river and then kiss and make up. Maybe it will be different this time, but let's don't count on it till it happens."

When Eddie caught his breath he answered, "Yes, I understand that. But there *is* more to it. Listen to what Mr. Fremont says."

John C. Fremont's Address
Free State Convention, Cleveland, Ohio:

Honored delegates of this Free State Convention, let me begin by commending Mr. Lincoln for his observation that I was born a Southerner, with as much affection for that section of the Union as I have for any other. I was raised in Charleston and tutored by an elder generation of Southerners who felt that slavery must be extinguished at some time in the future, but nevertheless is a practical necessity for the present.

We do not seek to antagonize the Southern people by denigrating them or their institutions. We ask only that they respect the wishes of our Founders, as Mr. Lincoln has so eloquently expressed them, that slavery be placed in such a position that the public mind will rest in the belief that it is set upon its course of ultimate extinction.

We are assembled here because President-elect Douglas has presented us with solid grounds for believing that it is his intention to set slavery on a foundation of permanence by spreading it to our Western Territories; by strengthening its grip on our existing Free States; and by spreading it to Mexico and other countries where it has long been extinguished.

He has given us reason to believe that he intends to preside over the acquisition of Mexico without the consent of Congress, for the purpose of admitting it to the Union as Slave States. He gives us sound reason to believe that he intends, on the basis of the controversial *Dred Scott Decision*, to strengthen the grip of slavery in the Free States though an aggressive enforcement of the Fugitive Slave Laws, to the extent of sending Negro-hunting expeditions into the North to put into chains all Negroes, including those who have long resided as free men and women.

What, then, should be our response to these provocations? In order that no one should be able with credibility to accuse us of disloyalty to our

Constitution and our government, I suggest that we respond to the President-elect's provocations by adopting his own methods:

President-elect Douglas is the author of the doctrine he calls Popular Sovereignty. Popular Sovereignty, as he explains it, is the doctrine that the settlers in any territory may choose to either abide by or ignore the laws on slavery, including the *Dred Scott Decision*.

Very well, then. Let us adopt Douglas' doctrine that each person may decide for himself how far to go in complying with the *Dred Scott Decision* and the Fugitive Slave Laws. Let us abide only by those our conscience tells us are just.

My conscience tells me that if slave catchers are in hot pursuit of runaway slaves who are obvious fugitives, then I must neither assist the slave catchers nor interfere with their pursuit of runaway slaves. But if the slave catchers come across the Ohio River with the intent of kidnapping any random Negroes they may by chance encounter, then it is my duty to protect the Negroes even to the point of resisting their would-be kidnappers.

I am advising this convention to adopt this resolution that the citizens of the Free States may be governed by their own consciences in deciding their compliance with the Fugitive Slave Laws; in particular, that they shall give neither aid nor hindrance to the hot pursuit of fugitive slaves; but that they shall resist the kidnapping of free Negroes, including any who have lived in an actual state of freedom for a period of years.

Eddie put down the paper. "The last part is about resisting the kidnapping of free Negroes. That means us!"

"Well, I suppose it's a step in the right direction," acknowledged Emma. "But fancy talk by itself don't amount to a hill of beans. I *might* believe those high-sounding words if and when the Free State *governments* band together and decide to *do* something to protect us." She contemplated the novel idea. "If they do, we might find ourselves at war with President Douglas and the Slave Power. Wouldn't *that* be something, this country going to war to free the Negroes instead of doing everything it can to keep us down?"

11

Montgomery County, Alabama, December 20, 1860

William Yancey

"Thanks for dropping by," William Yancey said in his silkiest tone.

"The pleasure's all mine," Jefferson Buford replied, entering Yancey's parlor. "What can I do you for?"

Yancey clasped his friend's hand firmly. "Well, I've been thinking it's about time we taught those Yankee Abolitionists a lesson, and you're just the man who can help me do it."

"Don't know about that, Bill. The Yankees can be mighty damn stubborn. What sort of lesson do you have in mind?"

Buford was wary, having locked horns with the Yankees up in 'Bleeding Kansas' and come off the worse for it. In 1856 Yancey and his fellow Fire Eaters had financed a mission to send Buford and four hundred Southern militiamen into Kansas to "settle the Territory and bring it into the Union as a Slave State." Upon arriving Buford had discovered the Yankees every bit as determined to bring Kansas into the Union as a Free State. Although Buford was a law-abiding, even-tempered man, he had found it impossible to avoid violent encounters with the Free State men. Outnumbered and discouraged, his band had abandoned their mission. Most had returned to Alabama, but some had switched sides and stayed on in Kanas as Free State men.

Yancey motioned for Buford to be seated. "Please set a spell and I'll tell you what I have in mind." Yancey motioned his house slave to bring refreshments.

When the two were comfortably seated, Yancey came to the point. "You know we're going to be conquered by the Abolitionists unless we gather our courage to stop them in their tracks. You saw for yourself how the Yankees stole Kansas out from under us --- after Stephen Douglas said we could take our slaves there. Now he tells us Kansas must be admitted as a Free State."

"Nobody can say we didn't do our best to settle it with our people," responded Buford. "Four hundred men just weren't enough. The Yankees brought in forty thousand. I'm afraid Douglas is right about Kansas. It belongs to the Yankees now."

Yancey winced as if his comrade's concession of Kansas to the Yankees was a dagger driven into his heart. "I hope we may yet have a chance to set things right in Kansas," he replied after calming himself. "If it does enter the Union as a Free State we'll lose our claim to the territories west of it, with their gold and silver. Those losses would confirm our status as an inconsequential minority in the Union. In such a reduced status we could not survive."

Buford shrugged. "It may not be all that bad. We've got Douglas in the White House and Davis is there looking over his shoulder to keep him honest. I've heard the rumors, as I'm sure you have, that they're planning the conquest of Mexico using our Southern militias. Then they're supposed to move on into Cuba and Central America. If we get those territories then Kansas, Colorado, and Nevada don't much matter do they? Maybe we'd best give Douglas and Davis a chance to show what they can do."

Yancey had anticipated this response.

"Yes, I've heard the stories about Douglas planning to authorize the conquest of Mexico. Maybe he'll do it; maybe he won't. He changes his mind more often than the weather. He promised us Kansas then he took it away, didn't he? So who can say what he'll do about Mexico and the rest. It's like as not that when it comes time to put the cards on the table, he'll claim he never heard of any such plan."

"Might could be," said Buford as he took a swig of bourbon. "But what do you have in mind for us to do about it? Not another expedition to Kansas, I hope. That horse has left the stable."

Again, Yancey winced at the thought of giving up Kansas. "No, Jeff, not Kansas. This time we must pierce the Yankee Abolitionists to their hearts. We have to answer John Brown's Raid. We have to let them know that if they insist on coming into our territory to incite our slaves against us, then we will go into their territory and take back the slaves that are rightfully ours. We've got to teach them that their Cleveland Resolutions do not nullify the Fugitive Slave Act. We need to teach these lessons now, not only to the Yankee Abolitionists, but to Stephen Douglas. He needs to understand that if he refuses to keep the promises he made to us, then it will devolve upon us to execute them ourselves."

"Go ahead. I'm listening."

"I want you to go up to Cass County, Michigan and break up that nest the runaway Niggers have made up there. Make it clear that the Abolitionists can't protect them. I've had Lucas Conyers, our old friend from the Kansas Expedition, up there since last year identifying runaways. I've located and purchased titles of ownership to eight of 'em. I want you to recover as many as you can. I'll pay thirty thousand dollars to organize the expedition and a thousand dollar bonus for each of the scalawags you bring back. You can split it with your men any way you want."

Buford whistled. "That ought to be enough to attract some daring men!"

"Some of your old Kansas hands should be about ready for another adventure," agreed Yancey. "You won't need more than a couple dozen. Here's a list of the runaway Niggers up there I purchased titles for:"

Yancey handed Buford copies of titles to the Negroes. Buford read the list. "Let's see, now, there's an Eddie Bates on Section 11 of Calvin Township just outside Cassopolis. He lives with a woman named Emma Brown. Both runaways --- Emma from 1850 and Eddie from 1833. How did you ever come up with the titles on those two?"

Yancey laughed. "I hired clerks to search the court records of runaways in Kentucky, Virginia, Maryland, and Delaware. Bought the title to Eddie Bates from his master's family in Maryland. Located the title to Emma Brown from the Delaware probate court and purchased it from the heirs of her deceased owner's estate."

"Well, you are nothing if not thorough, Bill. What else we got here...says there's a 'Shad Lee,' a 'Lucy Lee,' and two pickaninnies on Section 29 of Calvin Township."

"They're a family of runaways from Kentucky. Ran off from Shelby County, just last year."

Buford went on, "Looks like we got a couple other buck Niggers on the loose up there. They're on section 29 too. They look to be long in the tooth. Adam Jones, born in 1811 and Zed Jones born in 1807. Are you sure you want those old Darkies? I'd think they'd be more trouble to you than they're worth, for all the work you'd get out of them."

"I especially want those," Yancey answered with a grin. "I want ever Nigger on the lam up there to know they'll never rest. I want 'em to know they'll be hunted until the day they die. And I want 'em to know that all that Abolitionist fire-and-brimstone coming out of Cleveland and Boston can't help them. Once a Nigger's born into slavery he's got to know there's no escaping it. The Abolitionists who want to steal our Niggers need to know it too."

Something troubled Buford. He couldn't quite put it into words, but it didn't feel right. He clasped his hands together, elbows on the table.

"It wouldn't be an easy operation, Bill, even with Lucas up there to lead us straight to 'em. Those Niggers are going to squeal like pigs at a slaughterhouse when they find out we're taking 'em back into slavery. We'll have to catch 'em, bind 'em and gag 'em, and then get 'em back across the Ohio before the Abolitionists know they're gone. It's about three hundred miles from the Michigan line to the Ohio, isn't it? A lot of the way is backwoods, but we'd still have to pass through towns full of Abolitionists. Some of them are right on the Ohio River. I don't know if it's even possible to get past them."

"It's your show, Jeff. Do it any way you think best. But here's the way Lucas recommends going about it." Yancey brought over his *County, Township, and Rail Road Map of Ohio, Indiana and Michigan* and spread it out on the table.

"Niggertown's here," Yancey said, pointing to Calvin Township southeast of Cassopolis. "It's a Nigger settlement called 'Ramptown.' These eight Niggers I want live a little bit out in the country around there, so you can take 'em without riling up their Quaker neighbors. They live in three shacks less'n a mile apart. Lucas says best thing to do is take 'em at sunrise. Chain 'em and gag 'em and throw 'em in the back of a covered wagon. Might want to confine 'em in coffins to keep 'em still."

Buford laughed. "Putting 'em in coffins **would** keep 'em quiet."

78

Yancey smiled and gestured, as if letting Buford in on cherished secret.

"Now comes the good part. Soon as the Niggers are discovered missing, the Abolitionists will barricade the roads. They'll be thinking you're going to try slipping around to the east of South Bend and Fort Wayne and then go down the Indiana/Ohio line, like those old Kentucky slave catchers used to do in the '40s. Instead of doing that, Lucas says the best thing is to take the Niggers twelve miles due west to the vicinity of Niles." Yancey traced the route on the map with his finger.

"Niles is the head of navigation on the St. Joseph River. Hire a steamer and have it waiting there. You'll want to make sure the captain isn't too curious about the cargo he'll be carrying. Spend what you have to hire one who'll keep his mouth shut."

Buford nodded.

"Run the wagons on to the boat and take 'em down the river and across Lake Michigan to Michigan City, Indiana," Yancey explained. He pointed again at the map. "After you unload at Michigan City, Lucas will stay on the boat and see to it that the captain takes it to Milwaukee. Keeping the captain and the crew on the water will make sure they don't talk to anybody until your men and the Niggers are across the Ohio.

"From Michigan City drive the wagons down the road to Winamac. That's the Pulaski County Seat on the Tippecanoe River. It's about fifty miles. The Tippecanoe's not navigable for steamboats, but you can buy a flatboat and ride it to the Wabash and Ohio. Break down your wagons and stow 'em on board. When you get across the Ohio and back to Kentucky try to keep the Niggers under wraps as long as you can."

Yancey waved his arms expansively. "We want an air of mystery to surround this operation. The Niggers disappear out of Michigan. Nobody sees who took 'em. They show up here. Nobody knows how they got here. That'll make the runaway Niggers and their Abolitionist friends nervous as cats on a porch full of rockers."

"It looks like you've got this thing all figured out," Buford acknowledged. "If I agree to lead the operation it'll be best to wait for the weather to clear up in spring. I'll go up in March and talk to Lucas. If it looks like we can take the Niggers, I'll come back down and see who I can round up to go back with me in May."

79

"That's what I had in mind," said Yancey, raising his glass as if making a toast. "You see, great minds think alike."

Something still bothered Buford. "I've got to be honest with you. I don't especially like the idea of catching Niggers that have been running free all these years. When they're brought back to the plantation, they're so insolent you have to beat the work out of them. It's not worth it, and it sets a bad example for the other Niggers. I understand you want to recapture those Niggers to prove your point about Yankees having to obey the Fugitive Slave Law, but I don't know if that's the right way to go about it."

Yancey smiled. "I don't care a whit about keeping those goldbricking Niggers as slaves. The Yankee Abolitionists can buy them back from me if they want to and then set them free legally. That's all I'm asking. If the Yankees want these Negroes free, buy them and emancipate them legally. If the Yankees won't put up any of their money, then they'll show themselves to be the hypocritical old busybodies they are --- people who talk a good game about wanting our Niggers to be free, but who won't spend a dime of their own money buying their freedom."

"I see what you're trying to do," said Buford. "Teach the Niggers that the Abolitionists can't protect them. You're not really worried so much about recovering these particular slaves as you are about teaching the rest of 'em that it's senseless for them to try running away."

"That's exactly it!" exclaimed Yancey. "Put an end to the Abolitionists thinking that they can talk our Niggers into running away by promising to protect them."

"Makes perfect sense," agreed Buford. "It might just put an end to the trouble."

Yancey relaxed as Buford became agreeable to the plan. "Tell you something else, Jeff. You bring these Niggers back and I'll send you up next time to bring back old Fred Douglass. Wouldn't he be a prize! Let's see how much the Yankee Abolitionists will pay to get him back!"

Buford laughed and finished his bourbon. "Wouldn't that be something, to bring Fred Douglass down here and put him to work as a house servant? That might be the first worthwhile thing the old goat's ever done!"

12

Washington City, March 4th, 1861

Outgoing President James Buchanan and President-elect Stephen Arnold Douglas rode in an open carriage in the inaugural procession down Pennsylvania Avenue to the Capitol. "Old Buck" Buchanan felt the weight of the nation's troubles lifting off his shoulders. Sectional strife during his term had often made him wonder if he would be the last President of the United States. Now Douglas was coming into the office, having outsmarted those crazy Southern Fire Eaters in Charleston. As President, he could be expected to brook no defiance from the crazy Abolitionists either.

"The nation is most fortuitous to have chosen you as President," said Buchanan, feeling carefree for the first since becoming President. "I'll go home in peace, knowing the ship of state is being steered by a firm hand."

Douglas, who had been waving to the crowd, patted Old Buck on the shoulder. "You steered the ship safely into harbor during a heavy storm," he said absent-mindedly. "I hope and expect that our beloved 'Ship of state' shall find fairer weather on our next journey." Then he looked Old Buck in the eye and said sincerely, "Thank you, Sir, for doing all that was humanly possible in keeping our country united during a difficult time. Let me assure you most earnestly that henceforth our nation will be governed on a firm footing."

With that exchange, Buchanan sensed the nation's future had shifted, as if on a pivot. The nation *would* be placed on a firmer footing with Douglas at the helm. Buchanan sensed the "firmer footing" involved much more than settling the controversy over slavery. In Douglas he could sense a renewal of the old familiar America he had grown up with, not so much turning back of the clock to a simpler time, but more as a commitment to maintaining a familiar course into the future. There would be no lurching off into the newfangled and untried directions the younger and more energetic Republicans wanted to foist upon the nation.

Horace Greeley, editor of the *New York Tribune*, was thinking along those same lines as he followed behind in the newspaper owners' carriage, busily taking notes on the proceedings. Greeley supported the Republicans, but moderate in his views and not especially opposed to Union-minded Democrats like Stephen Douglas and Jefferson Davis. He had taken a liking to Davis, having met him in New York during his recent speaking tour urging Northerners to have patience with the Confederate Union, while giving the Douglas Administration a fair hearing.

Nevertheless, Greeley was discomfited by the election of Douglas and Davis for the same reasons Democrats like Buchanan were relieved. He fretted that the cause of Emancipation would be set back, though he had never expected it to happen in his lifetime under any administration. But there was more to it than that. He searched his mind diligently. What was the real, essential difference between the Republicans and Democrats?

Part of it, he supposed, was the youthful energy the Republicans had campaigned with. In the North they had won the allegiance of the younger, better educated, and more prosperous voters. They seemed oriented towards the future. They spoke plenty about containing slavery, but many Republicans, perhaps even most of them, weren't fanatical about it. They had a one-sentence summary of the issue: "Let slavery alone where it already is, so long as it expands no further." They seemed to regard it as a secondary issue; block it from expanding, prevent it from dominating the nation, then move on to other issues.

Those "other issues" had something to do with progressive social movements like granting women the right to vote and to own property in their own names. Part of it was a more open-minded view of sexuality. The younger Republicans, at least the more sophisticated ones, might be caught whispering about "open marriages, free love" and other scandalous topics. They talked a lot about religion and philosophy. Some were intellectual theologians while others were militant atheists. They also liked to discuss scientific discoveries in all fields of human knowledge.

The business-oriented among them talked about their expansive dreams of building great new commercial empires, of flooding the world with American made products so as to create prosperity at home and abroad. They had their eyes especially on the "golden lands of the East" beyond the California coastline.

They were keen to develop new markets for American products among Asia's uncounted millions. They were indifferent to territorial expansion, saying, "We desire no more territory from Mexico. We would rather prosper by investing our surplus capital in building its railroads and seaports." They seemed to want the United States to become a sort of Greater British Empire, making the country powerful and prosperous through global commerce. They wanted to be accepted into the European-dominated club of Great Powers rather than provoke European hostility.

The Democrats, in contrast, seemed much more tradition-bound. Democrats were plain folks like farmers, mechanics, and small-town merchants. Greeley didn't think they were less intelligent than Republicans, but their horizons seemed less broad. They were traditional in their family values. They considered divorce, let alone free love, scandalous. They went to church, or didn't go, without trying to intellectualize the reasons. Their concept of "creating a commercial empire" was about becoming the biggest dry goods merchant in town.

Greeley began to understand that there was more than just a moral difference between Republicans and Democrats on the question of slavery. He perceived that Democrats endorsed slavery because it was what they were familiar with. Their fathers, grandfathers, and great grandfathers had owned slaves, so why shouldn't they and their sons and grandsons? Slavery had always been part of the Southern way of life and it always would be. That was never going to change.

Republicans knew that things *would* change, that they were going to change rapidly in new and unexpected directions. Greeley had heard and read Lincoln's many speeches about industrial and engineering topics. He knew Lincoln was an inventor who owned a patent for steamboat propulsion. He knew of Lincoln's enthusiasm for the invention of machinery that would multiply the productivity of labor by a thousand-fold and thereby create fantastic wealth for the masses.

Lincoln, like other Republicans, seemed to have an eye open to the future when America would become a land of great cities and industries, bound to every part of the world by commerce and instantaneous telegraph communications. Could plantation slavery continue to exist in this mechanized world? Could millions of Negroes be held down in ignorance and poverty when the ability of Man to disseminate knowledge and wealth was accelerating? Greeley gained a sudden insight into Lincoln's mind: that the Abolitionists didn't have to eliminate slavery all by themselves. Progress would kill it for them, *if* the Republicans kept the nation true to its founding principles that all men were created equal.

He gleaned insight into the minds of Southern Fire Eaters as well. They saw the future too, even if less clearly than the Republicans. They understood that the increase of communications and the spreading of wealth would one day make it impossible for them to control their Negroes, unless they subverted the founding principles of the country. They must make the people believe the country was established on the principle of racial hierarchy sanctifying the "right" of peoples of European ancestry to enslave the dark-skinned races.

He began to understand the workings of Stephen Douglas' mind. He surmised that Douglas did not hate Negroes, or even believe they were inferior beings. Douglas was simply indifferent to them. He was just as indifferent to the State of Massachusetts granting full civil rights to Negroes, including their right to vote, as he was indifferent to the State of Virginia enslaving them, or of Illinois constraining their freedom with vagrancy laws. He saw nothing unusual about living in a country where the laws of some states were based on equality and the laws of others were based on slavery. Douglas didn't care, so long as the country remained united under one flag and continued to expand.

Douglas seemed rather like a real estate speculator bent on parceling out North America into subdivisions of Free States and Slave States. His talk of "Confederate Union" implied a looser, but also more extended Confederation that would grow to encompass Mexico and Central America, the Canadas, and much of the Caribbean. Douglas didn't seem to care much what went on inside all these "houses" as long as they hung the American flag from their porches.

Douglas' vision of this Confederate Union unsettled Greeley. He didn't covet Canada with its French population and allegiance to the Queen. He thought of Mexico as an arid desert. Cuba was productive of sugar, but the United States already had sources of sugar inside its current borders. He felt that Douglas would run the risk of involving the United States in costly wars to obtain these marginal territories. Perhaps Douglas would cause the United States to antagonize the rest of the world by appearing to be an uncivilized nation bent on spreading slavery by conquest.

Beyond that, as a practical matter, Greeley wondered whether Douglas' concept of national government would be adequate to administer a nation looking forward to a new century of progress. Could the United States continue to be governed as a Confederation of Sovereign States with each state master of its own domestic laws? Could each state continue to be sovereign over interstate commerce and railroads? Greeley sensed that the national government would soon be compelled to assert its supremacy over the hodgepodge of conflicting state laws impeding the nation's commerce. Douglas' idea of a sprawling continent-wide Confederation of States, each state sovereign in citizenship and law, did not seem compatible with the nation's future development.

Greeley decided he would try to influence Douglas rather than antagonize him with partisan complaints. He would orient his paper's coverage of the inauguration around the theme that Douglas should be receptive to the Republican ideas on economic progress while getting on with the main business of fairly dividing the United States into Slave States and Free States.

He would editorialize that Douglas had the opportunity to become one of the great American Presidents, in the tradition of George Washington, if he recognized that state governments were the supreme instruments of civil governance, while the Federal Government must be recognized as the supreme instrument of national economic governance. Greeley thought that idea over and liked it. Maybe all would yet be well with Douglas having his romp in Mexico and the Canadas --- if he could also be persuaded to work with the Republicans in Congress to strengthen the federal authority over business law. Let the Democrats have their land and slaves, and the Republicans have their industry and commerce!

While Greeley penned the outline of his article the procession continued down Pennsylvania Avenue to the Capitol. There the Presidential party stopped at the Senate Chamber. Buchanan's outgoing Vice President John Breckinridge warmly embraced his friend Jefferson Davis. Before taking his oath as Vice President, Davis gave a speech reaffirming his devotion to the entire Confederate Union, including his affection for the New England States and the "rising states" of the Northwest and California. "All states, old and new, North and South, East and West, are valued residents of our House of Confederate Union."

Greeley noted that for the moment relations between the North and South didn't appear particularly hostile. Tennessee Senator Andrew Johnson, soon to be the Postmaster General in Douglas' Cabinet, stood off in the corner gossiping with New York Senator William Seward. Johnson pulled out a flask of his ever present "medicinal whiskey" and shared it with Seward, then began telling a story. Judging by the expression on Seward's face it was probably ribald.

President-elect Douglas saw the flask and made a beeline for it, grabbing the whiskey out of Johnson's hands and taking a giant snort. He winced playfully at Johnson, perhaps inferring that the whiskey was crudely made moonshine. The three kept laughing and passing the flask around while Jefferson Davis droned on from the podium.

Davis finished and took the oath of office. The audience in the Senate Chamber then followed Douglas outside the Capitol and stood before a crowd of tens of thousands. Before taking the oath of office Douglas gave his inaugural speech. The sun parted as Douglas passed his hat to Davis. Douglas spoke in the windy sunlight.

Fellow-Citizens of the Confederate Union:

I appear before you to take the office of President. I will follow the precedent of giving a brief Inaugural Address for the purpose of vindicating the course which it will be my duty to pursue upon the great public questions now before the country.

Our paramount duty at this time must be to defend our Confederate Union from assault by foes external and internal.

In the external sphere we have learned of the design by certain European Powers to extend a hegemonic empire over our Continent. The seat of their Empire is to be Mexico. Their pretext for usurping the Mexican Republic is the alleged state of disorder in that country, a result of the ongoing conflict between Reformers and Conservatives, which is said not only to be an affront to civilization but to have caused the default of Mexico's debt obligations.

I do not need to tell you that this usurpation of the government and territory of a North American Republic is a trespass upon the Monroe Doctrine, an insult to the American people, and a threat to the interests of the Confederate Union of States, which are destined by Providence to become coextensive with the Northern Continent. The Confederate Union is sovereign upon this continent and cannot allow for the encroachment of a foreign power upon any inch of its soil.

To prevent their acquisition by an alien power we hereby invite the Republic of Mexico to enter into our Confederate Union. We also invite the Dominions of British North America into our Union, and I ask Congress to appropriate such sum as will be considered fair compensation for our purchase of said Dominions.

Let me turn now to those domestic mischief-makers who are continuing to sow discord by their unceasing agitation over slavery.

This Confederate Union can only be preserved by maintaining the fraternal feeling between the North and the South, the East and the West. If that good feeling can be preserved, the Union will be as perpetual as the fame of its great founders. It **can** be maintained by preserving the sovereignty of the States, the right of each State and each Territory to settle its domestic concerns for itself, and the duty of each to refrain from interfering with the other in any of its local or domestic institutions. Let that be done, and the Union will be perpetual; let that be done, and this Republic, which began with thirteen States, and which now numbers thirty-three, which, when it began, only extended from the Atlantic to the Mississippi, but now reaches to the Pacific, may yet expand North and South, until it covers the whole Continent, and becomes one vast ocean-bound confederacy.

But certain Abolitionists desire the destruction of this great Republic. They have invited a war of the North against the South, warfare of the Free States against the slaveholding States.

And why? Because they say the Declaration of Independence contains this language: "We hold these truths to be self-evident, that all men are created equal; that they are endowed by their Creator with certain inalienable rights; that among these are life, liberty and the pursuit of happiness." Then they declare that "all men" includes Negroes.

I confess to you, my fellow-citizens, that I am utterly opposed to that system of Abolition philosophy. The signers of the Declaration of Independence were speaking of the White race, the European race on this continent, and their descendants, and emigrants who should come here. They were speaking only of the White Race, and never dreamed that their language would be used in an attempt to make this nation a mixed nation of Indians, Negroes, Whites, and Mongrels.

This was the great issue of the recent election. The result is there for all to see. We will expect the Free States to honor the Constitution and to comply with their obligation thereunder to honor in all its particulars the Fugitive Slave Laws, as nobly as they have complied with all the other laws of the land.

My friends, the path of duty, of honor, of patriotism, is plain. We have established this Confederate Union on the fundamental basis of State Sovereignty, the right of each State to decide for itself the character of its domestic institution without interference or imposition from any other state. Bear in mind the dividing line between State rights and Federal authority; let us maintain the great principles of sovereignty, of State rights, and of the Confederate Union as the Constitution has made it, and this Republic will endure forever. We will maintain domestic tranquility while expanding our boundaries from the center of this continent to the oceans that surround it.

Confederate Union, United Expansion!

13

2nd Cleveland Convention, March 27, 1861

Abraham Lincoln   John Fremont

Abraham Lincoln was enjoying after-dinner tea with John Fremont, Congressman John Sherman, Senator William Seward, and William Lloyd Garrison in a quiet anteroom set back from the Weddell House's main dining room. They were the Second Free State Convention's Platform Committee --- the committee of five chosen by the delegates to decide how the convention would represent itself to the nation and the world.

This Second Free State Convention was more formal than the first. Every Free State Governor, except the Democrats elected in Illinois, Indiana, California, and Oregon, were in attendance, as were many Republican Senators and Congressmen, and Republican newspaper owners. Thousands of Wide Awakes loitered around the edges of the convention, singing Republican campaign songs and marching in torchlight processions.

This convention had been called in response to Douglas' *Declaration of Protection of Mexico* --- his euphemism for the preemptive military conquest of Mexico before the French arrived there in force. French Emperor Napoleon III had ordered his fleet to seize the port of Vera Cruz, ostensibly to collect customs duties in lieu of the payments in arrears on his Mexican bonds. Now his army had begun debarking the numbers required for marching up the well-travelled invasion route into Mexico City, first used by Conquistadors in the 1500's and recently by Americans in 1847. Douglas intended to preempt him by annexing Mexico, as he'd promised Davis.

"We've got to side with Douglas on this one," insisted Seward. "The Monroe Doctrine is a national issue that rises above partisanship. We need to show the people that our party is as patriotic in its defense as any Douglas Democrat."

"Then let Douglas present Congress with a proper declaration of war," retorted Congressman Sherman. "You know full well that he's devolving the war on to the states because he knows we'll never approve his scheme to annex Mexico as Slave States."

Seward piddled with his cup. "He's promised to get us the Canadas after he's done with Mexico. The Canadas will augment the Free States more than Mexico will augment the Slave States. Perhaps we should keep our silence about Mexico."

"You're missing the point!" exclaimed Sherman, nearly shouting. "Neither the Mexicans or the Canadians have volunteered to be Americans! And Congress sure as hell hasn't approved a war to conquer them and bring them into the country against their will!"

Fremont milling around nearby put his hand on Seward's shoulder. "We can't let Douglas turn this whole country over to slavery, even if he promises us Heaven itself. We must draft resolutions disavowing our participation in the Mexican scheme. We must let Douglas know that under no circumstances will we allow the *Dred Scott Decision* to be construed as a license for slave raids into the Free States. We need to draft these resolutions and get them to the Free State legislatures for ratification. Otherwise, there's no reason for Douglas to take us seriously."

Lincoln put down his cup. "Let's not be in such a hurry to kick Douglas in the pants when he's about to stumble over his untied shoelaces! Let's see if he backs down from his Mexican adventure, now that the Europeans are warning him that Mexico is their province, and they'll fight if he attempts to annex it. If he backs down, he'll look foolish enough without us saying a word. If he chooses war, he'll bankrupt every Slave State trying to pay for it. The Europeans may humiliate him by blockading the Slave State ports, and perhaps seizing them. Let's just make sure that everybody in our party understands why we can't vote to fund the war from the national Treasury. Douglas says it's a Slave State war. Then let the Slave States bear the cost of it. But let's not provoke them with resolutions of defiance."

"Douglas is a sneaky son of a bitch," replied Fremont. "You know he's going to use the war to whip up a patriotic fervor to drive us out of office in '62. After he gets rid of us he'll ask Congress to assume the Slave States' war debts. If we don't oppose him now, we won't be able to later."

Lincoln, deep in thought, stood up with his cup of hot tea, opened the door, and walked into the dining room. He noticed the poetic plaque on the wall:

Man's life is like a Winter's day;
Some only breakfast and away;
Others to dinner stay and are well fed
The oldest but sups and goes to bed,
Long is his life who lingers out the day
Who goest soonest has the least to pay.
Tho' I owed much, I hope long trust is given,
And truly mean to pay all bills in Heaven.

The playful poem put him in good humor. He suddenly thought of a story that might persuade Fremont and Garrison to soften their position. He came back into the anteroom and sat back down. Leaning back in his chair he started the story: "Our situation reminds me of a party of Methodist parsons from the country who were travelling together to Chicago."

The other men leaned forward in anticipation of another of Lincoln's stories, often told in a backwoods vernacular making them all the funnier. Lincoln acknowledged their attention with a wink and resumed telling the story with gusto.

"Well, they got to Springfield ten minutes after the afternoon train left the station. For three hours two of the parsons set there discussin' and considerin' how to get to Chicago. One favored buyin' a flatboat and paddlin' up the river while another favored goin' back to git their horses and makin' a ride of it. One of the parsons remained silent all through this tedious debate. Finally, one of the others asked, 'What say you, Brother Joseph?' Brother Joseph answered, 'I say we wait rat here fer the evenin' train.'"

The men laughed.

"Abe, you **should** have been elected President!" exclaimed Fremont. "Lord knows, the people would enjoy a man with a sense of humor in that capital of pompous bigheads."

Seward gulped his rum-stiffened tea then laughed. "Now, John, you wouldn't be including yourself in that crowd of bigheads, would you?"

The men roared with laughter. Fremont, whose explorations had gone a long way toward winning the West, had an ego every bit as large as the territories he had done so much to acquire for the United States. His delight in pomp and pageantry annoyed his colleagues from California to Washington City but were a part of his popular mystique. His accent mixed the Southern dialect of Savannah and Charleston, where he was raised, with the French he'd picked up from his French-Canadian father, and hist later travels in Europe. Though widely regarded as a Yankee Abolitionist, his demeanor hinted of the South, the West, the Northwest, and even European royalty. Fremont's worldliness complemented Lincoln's backwoods wit.

Though easily offended, Fremont seemed to take Lincoln's and Seward's comments in good humor. "A wonderful story, Abe, but poignant as it was, it nevertheless has a deficiency. The deficiency is that the 1864 'train' will not have room for us. It will be fully booked by Democrats."

"Why should that be?" Lincoln asked. "We fell only a few thousand votes short in Illinois and Indiana this time around. The way our population is growing, we'll have seventy-five thousand new voters in Illinois and twenty-five in Indiana in '64. Those will mostly be our voters. They will take us straight to the White House."

"Think again," implored Fremont. "Why do you suppose California and Oregon voted against us two-to-one? We lost as much because of them as because of Illinois or Indiana. California and Oregon don't have a single slave owner and yet they vote the same as South Carolina or Mississippi. Why do you think that is?"

"I'd hazard a guess it's because the territorial governors were appointed by Polk and Pierce," explained Lincoln. "They had plenty of time to pack the territorial governments with Southern Democrats who influenced the votes of the first settlers. But now that you mention it, I expect that California and Oregon will be voting with us soon too. There will surely be more Free State emigrants into those territories than Slave State men."

"It won't be like that," insisted Fremont shaking his head. By now the others were following the conversation with interest. "Let me ask you: where are your new immigrant voters in Illinois coming from?"

"Well.....mostly from where you'd expect. New York, New England, Pennsylvania. Some from Ohio. And there's the Dutch."

"And what do these immigrants do when they arrive?" asked Fremont.

"They clear the land and build farms, most of them do."

"And how much unsettled land is there left in Illinois?"

"Not as much as there used to be," said Lincoln, suddenly beginning to feel uncomfortable. "There's still untilled land available for purchase up around Galena. Not the best land by a long shot, but workable. There's still some patches of untilled land from Springfield to the Mississippi and south of there. Again, not the best land, but productive enough for those willing to do the work. But I see your point. The best lands, especially in eastern and central Illinois are settled."

"And who's going to come into Illinois when the last of the unsettled land is occupied?"

Lincoln paused to think about that. The untilled farmland in Illinois *would* be gone in ten years, if it lasted that long. While Chicago's growth would continue attracting new settlers into the state.

"The manufactories, railroads, and commercial enterprises in Chicago are accepting the labor of all who apply," Lincoln replied. "Any man who gets off the morning train can be gainfully employed by afternoon."

"And how do these laborers in Chicago vote?"

Lincoln paused again. "Most of them vote..."

John Sherman finished the sentence. "That's right, Abe, most vote Democratic. I see what John is getting at. The country's changing. We won't be a nation of farmers much longer. We've built some large industrial combinations employing thousands of laborers. Just look around you here in Cleveland. What do you see? Factories and mills. The owners are Republicans. The workers aren't."

Seward sighed. "That's true in New York as well. The way New York City is growing, I don't know if we'll be able to hold the state much longer. Lots of Irishmen are arriving in Boston too. Let me tell you, they're no friends of Republicans or Negroes. They say, 'A Negro will do any job for less than a White man.' The Democrats have really set their hooks into those people. They've convinced them that Negroes are only interested in taking their jobs and marrying their daughters. They tell them we're the party of 'Nigger equality.'"

"Out in California we don't get the immigrant vote either," seconded Fremont. "We've got a lot of Italians in San Francisco. Most are Democrats. The Southerners who came in with the territorial governments taught them to despise Republicans and Negroes. And don't think that Douglas won't be appointing his Southern friends to the territorial governments in Colorado, Utah, New Mexico, and the territories that will be split off from Nebraska. He'll turn those territories into Democrat fiefdoms too. They'll pin us back into the Northeast, then they'll turn our industrial workers against us. If we don't act now to get ourselves out from under those people, it will be too late. We can't wait until 1864."

"Is it really that bad, John?" Lincoln asked. "After all, you're from Charleston, the very center of the Southern Rights movement. You weren't deceived by their anti-Negro propaganda."

"That was another era, Abe. When I was a young cub, Charleston was a Federalist City, like Boston. We believed that Abolition was inevitable. It was only later on that Charleston, like the rest of the South, became hardline on slavery. Don't you see, gentlemen, that this is where we're headed as a country! The Supreme Court has ruled that slaves may be carried into any state! My heavens, who would have believed just a few years ago that *any* court in the land would commit such an outrage? Now Davis and Douglas are in the White House with the power to appoint territorial governors and federal judges. They will turn this entire country against us. We won't even be secure in the North, at least not anywhere other than New England."

"So, what are you suggesting we do, John?" asked Congressman Sherman. "You might as well come right out and say it."

Fremont whispered quietly so no one outside the room could hear:

"Gentlemen, the ultimate question before us is nothing more or less than whether the Free States will remain free by combining together as a separate national sovereignty." The men appeared relieved that Fremont had spoken what they were all thinking. "We can't answer that question now. But we can let the people know that we've raised it so they can begin to consider it.

"We should send the resolutions that Garrison and I have drafted to the Free State legislatures for their consideration. That will fire the hearts of our Free State citizens with the idea that the time may come when the Free States must join together to preserve our rights as free men. We also should establish a permanent character for this convention so that Douglas and Davis will not view it as a temporary expression of grievance. I propose that each state should select a delegate who will stay on as our permanent coordinating committee. The committee will have authority to reconvene this full convention if conditions warrant." Fremont looked at Lincoln to gauge his reaction.

Lincoln rubbed his chin and closed his eyes. The foundations of his political views were the histories he had read of George Washington urging the states to set aside their differences and unite under a common national government. He envisioned a future United States united in prosperity and freedom, slavery extinguished by the consent of its people. He believed that subdividing the Union would be treasonous. Yet he began to see that a suffocating government might be imposed by the Confederate Union. Perhaps the light of liberty would be snuffed out in the Free States before it could illuminate the Slave States.

*This involves more than just slavery. Douglas has said in his inaugural address that the Chinese, Japanese, Indians, Negroes, and all other "inferior races" are destined to be forever excluded from citizenship and civil rights. He says we are to become a racially organized nation with the Whites on top and the colored peoples on bottom. He wants to conquer Mexico and convert it into a New South peopled by white plantation owners, Negro slaves, and Mexican peons. His Democratic Party will be busy in the North indoctrinating every immigrant workingman to despise Negroes, Mexicans, and all those other 'inferior races.' Under his administration the United States will recede from the Civilized Nations. It will become an isolated and belligerent power imposing slavery on free nations. **I will have no part of it!***

He opened his eyes and sat upright. Then he folded his hands together and leaned forward towering over the table.

"In light of John's persuasive arguments, I withdraw my objection to this convention going on record with the resolutions that he and Garrison have proposed. I also have no objection to establishing a permanent character to the coordinating committee as he proposes."

14

Charleston, South Carolina, April 11, 1861

"Douglas got his wings clipped, but good this time." William Yancey laughed gleefully. "The old double-crossing buzzard will never fly again." He waved the front page of the latest edition of *The New York Tribune* to reach Charleston:

European Proclamation on Containment of Slavery!

From London, England, March 26. The foreign ministers of the governments of Great Britain, France, and Spain have today issued a *Joint Proclamation on Containment of Slavery* warning that any intervention by the Slave-Holding States of America into Mexico will be met with a joint declaration of war. Britain's foreign minister also declined the request by President Douglas to enter into discussions for the sale of its North American Possessions.

Republican Free State Convention to Issue Resolutions

From Cleveland, O., March 29. The Platform Committee of the Second Free State Convention is drafting resolutions to be voted on by the full Convention and, if approved, to be recommended to the Free State Legislatures.

Said John C. Fremont, President of the Convention:

"The citizens of the Free States will be guided by President Douglas' very own Doctrine of Popular Sovereignty declaring that in regard to slavery the citizens of each locality shall determine for themselves which Acts of Congress and Supreme Court Rulings that they shall be bound to comply with. We will contribute neither manpower nor financial support to the reckless misadventures of the Douglas / Davis Administration in seeking to spread slavery into Mexico. Nor will we allow the Supreme Court to graft slavery onto the Free States by its excessive ruling in *Dred Scott vs. Sanford.*"

Robert Barnwell Rhett, publisher of the influential *Charleston Mercury* guffawed. "He damn well got his tail feathers shorn too, by both the Europeans and the Free Staters. You'd think he'd of learned by now that the Free Staters are going to keep turning his crazy ideas on Popular Sovereignty against him."

Yancey and Rhett sat in the sloppy clutter of Rhett's editorial office. Like newspaper offices everywhere, every nook and cranny was stuffed with faded yellow papers from years past.

"That's not anywhere near the worst of it," replied Yancey, continuing to read from the newspaper account. "The Free Staters are coordinating with the British. Judging by the date of the European Proclamation the British knew weeks in advance that Fremont was going to stand with them against our acquisition of Mexico. Making common cause with a foreign power is treason in my book."

"It certainly is," agreed Rhett, sitting back lazily and throwing his feet over the footstool. "I don't think the Europeans would have been so bold if Fremont hadn't told them that the Free States were with them. You know, I'm generally well disposed toward the Brits, but I'm not sure I like them telling us what we can and can't do on our own continent. Can't say as I blame them for wanting to keep the Canadas, but Mexico is in our bailiwick. They sure as shootin' turned the Monroe Doctrine against us on that one."

Yancey threw down the paper. "I wonder how Davis feels about being tricked into throwing in with Douglas. If he'd listened to us, he'd be president of our Southern Republic, not sitting with his pants down in Douglas' outhouse."

Rhett rolled his eyes. "About all we can hope for now is that Douglas kicks the bucket, then maybe we'll be able to talk some sense into Davis. I don't fancy sitting here on our rear ends, counting the days until the liver-spotted old jackass dies. Hell, he might live 'til the Second Coming for all we know."

Yancey drew a sly smile as the conversation moved in the direction he anticipated. "Bob, now's the time for me to let you in on a project I've been brewing since late last year. I would have told you about it sooner, but I didn't know for sure if it would be worth pursuing. It makes perfect sense now, with the British and French checkmating Douglas, and with the Free States agitating in his rear."

Rhett perked up in his chair. "What do you have under your hat?"

"I'm thinking of sending Jeff Buford and a couple dozen of his best men into Michigan to recover some runaway slaves. I've purchased title to the slaves, so legally they're mine. I've given him a plan to ferry the slaves across Lake Michigan into Indiana then get them down the Wabash to Kentucky. The Yankees will be looking for him everywhere except there, so he's got a fair chance of getting back across the Ohio. I'd appreciate your help in financing this venture, if you think it's something you'd like to participate in."

"Hell, yes!" cried Rhett. "I'll write you a check faster than a bell clapper in a goose's ass. You know how much I'd love to tweak the Yankees by taking those Niggers out from under them. How much do you need?"

"I've committed thirty thousand dollars."

Yancey thought the tight-fisted newspaper editor was about to have a heart attack. Rhett gulped but proved true to his word. "How about if I front you five thousand? I'll ask my subscribers to kick in the rest when your men get back with the Niggers. Hell, they'll probably commit enough coin to fund this raid plus several more."

"Bet they will!" Yancey laughed. "I am much obliged." He leaned back and relaxed. "This raid is going to make the Yankees madder'n a wet hen in a jute bag. They'll likely try to declare their independence from our Confederate Union. One of two things will happen then. Douglas and Davis will either let them go, which means we'll be rid of them for good and all, or else they'll try to reclaim them. If they do, we'll go up there and kick their tails. We'll put our men in control of those states. We'll reconstruct them so they'll never bother us again. Doesn't matter to me which way it pans out, as long as we get the Republicans and Abolitionists out of our hair."

Rhett picked up on the thought. "I reckon the raid will be well worth our investment. With the Republicans and Abolitionists suppressed we'd be able to regain control of the West. We'd be able to bring our slaves into Kansas, Colorado, and Nevada. We could split California, like we should have done in 1850. There's good land in California we could turn into slave plantations. We could put a lot of Niggers to work on those gold and silver mines. Put 'em to work building railroads too. There'd be a lot of money to be made, for sure."

"Exactly," said Yancey. "Then, after we've taken the West, we'll be strong enough to stare down the European meddlers in Mexico. Hell, now that I think about it, I don't know if I even want Mexico any more, not if I can get our own Far West and California. Mexico's full of Greasers. We go in there and our boys will be marrying the senoritas. Next thing you know and we'll be mongrelized."

"The senoritas are liable to turn our boys into Catholics too," Rhett theorized, "and the Catholics are worse than Yankees when it comes to opposing slavery. We've had problems with a few of 'em agitating against slavery right here in Charleston."

"So maybe we better let the Greasers keep their country.....for now," Yancey agreed. "We'll take the West, all of it, away from the Yankees and then we'll figure a way to convince Spain it ought to sell us Cuba. The Brits can't very well object to us bringing slavery into a colony that already has it. We'll decide what to do about Mexico later on."

Rhett smirked. "Looks like that'll keep everybody happy. Let the French have Mexico for the time being. The British can keep their icebox in the Canadas. We'll get the West and then work on Cuba and maybe Mexico. Everybody'll be happy with *that* deal."

Yancey snorted. "Everybody 'cept the Damn Yankees!"

15

Cass County, Michigan, May 6, 1861

Eddie Bates came into the kitchen smiling at his wife Emma. The smell of her cooking bacon and eggs on the stove mixed with the fragrance of spring from the budding plants outside the open window. The sun was just below the horizon and the deep purple of pre-dawn rimmed the horizon.

Part of Eddie's cheer derived from the latest edition of the *North Star Liberator*.

"The 2nd Cleveland Convention done passed some powerful-sounding resolutions and sent them on to the Free State Legislatures for ratification," he told Emma. "You know, they kept those resolutions secret for thirty days so's the Free State Legislatures could consider them out of the public eye, but now the cat is out of the bag. Here they are:"

We, the citizens of the United States of Free America, in order to restore our country to its founding principle that all men are created equal and are endowed by their Creator with certain inalienable rights, do hereby solemnly and jointly declare the following resolutions:

1. Resolved, that all residents of the Free States are now and forever shall be free.

2. Resolved, that the so-called Fugitive Slave Laws are rendered nugatory by the application of Popular Sovereignty, the doctrine our current President defines as granting to each citizen the right to decide for himself whether to uphold or ignore the laws governing slavery. No citizen may be coerced into assisting with the return of any Free State resident to slavery.

3. Resolved, that citizens of the Free States may commit themselves to protecting Free State residents, including those of Color, and to resist their kidnapping and return to slavery by the agents of the Slave Power.

4. Resolved, that the citizens of the Free States will resist any and all attempts by the Slave Power to expand its territory through the instigation of wars of aggression against foreign nations, including, but not limited to, Mexico, Cuba, and the other Nations of the Caribbean and Central America.

"There's more, but those are the important ones."

Emma was still in her nightclothes. She was expecting to stay home and clean house as there was no need to accompany Eddie into the bakery they ran in Cassopolis today. The dogs in the yard started howling.

"Dogs barking up a storm," Emma said.

"Guess that ol' fox is back to making his mornin' rounds," Eddie replied.

Then the door burst open. Jefferson Buford and four of his men swarmed in.

Eddie's voice pitched high. He jumped up and shouted, "What do you mean bustin' in...." Before he could finish the men knocked him off his feet, rolled him over and cuffed his hands and feet with shackles.

"Shut up, Nigger," one of the men said. "You holler out again and I'll knock your candle out." He stuffed a rag in Eddie's mouth and tied it around his head.

For some reason she could not explain, Emma remained calm. Something inside her told her she must not lose her temper or appear frightened of these men. "Who are you men? What do you want with us?" she asked matter-of-factly.

Her calmly polite manner threw Buford off his stride. A practiced slave catcher would have bound and gagged Emma before she had a chance to open her mouth. But Buford had not captured runaway slaves before and his heart had not hardened to the task. He was torn between the ancient Southern dilemma of whether to regard slaves as property or human beings. Moreover, Emma was a light-skinned woman. Buford wondered if she had ever tried to "pass" herself as white. She probably could with slight effort to lighten her skin and bleach her hair. Instinctively he answered Emma with the courtesy he would speak to a white woman.

"We are here to recover runaway slaves, ma'am. I regret to say this includes you and your husband. There is no question about your being runaways. I have the papers proving it and if necessary, will use them to compel the sheriffs and federal marshals in these parts to assist me with your return to your lawful owner. Now please come along with us peaceably. We can hardly bear to think of using force on a woman, but the law allows it if we have to. Please don't make it necessary."

Eddie's stomach churned at these words. A minute ago, he'd walked in the fresh breath of freedom the Cleveland Convention had blown across the North; now he was destined to return to the degradation his father had brought him away from! Emma was to be returned to slavery too. For the first time, Eddie felt the slave's ultimate humiliation of being unable to protect his family. He and Emma might be sold to separate masters, might never see each other again. With a mind-numbing shock of recognition Eddie understood that his recurring nightmares of being returned to slavery had not been idle dreams.

Amidst this calamity Emma felt herself steadied by a power larger than herself.

"Well, sirs, if that's the way it has to be, then that's the way it has to be," she replied cordially. "Law's on your side. I'll come with you and won't make no fuss. Only thing is, I'm in my nightclothes. Please allow me a few minutes to get dressed, if'n you will. You don't want to bring back a woman who's caught pneumonia, I don't reckon. While I'm changing, you men are welcome to help yourselves to the breakfast that's cooking. No use letting it go to waste."

"Much obliged ma'am," said Buford, thankful for the cooperation. "Please be quick."

103

"This is one Nigger wench that talks sense," agreed one of his men. "Let's get our breakfast. I'm hungry." He opened the door and called to the other men watching outside to come in.

The men enjoyed their helpings of bacon and coffee. After a few minutes Buford noticed that Emma had not come out of her room. He knocked on her door. No answer. He knocked again, then shouted for her to come out. He opened the door. In the darkness he didn't see her. Nor did he see the outside door to the walk-through closet. By that time Emma was a half mile away, riding toward Sheriff Parker's office on the horse she had quietly let out of the barn.

Emma spurred the horse as she rode toward town. The Slavers, for all their bluster about Northern lawmen being compelled by the Fugitive Slave Act to help them, were already heading South as fast as they could go with Eddie, before the sheriffs could be alerted to rescue him. He might be beyond rescue if the Slavers had scouted out a backwoods route to get them to the Ohio River and across it into Kentucky before word of the kidnapping filtered into the Abolitionist communities.

She fought back tears knowing that not every person north of the Ohio River was like the people of Cass County. There were all too many Negro-haters between here and the Ohio who would gleefully assist the slave catchers in returning Eddie to slavery.

16

The White House, May 10, 1861

President Stephen Arnold Douglas took serious aim, but only part of his wad of chewing tobacco found its mark. The rest flew over the spittoon and embedded itself in the thick rug covering the Executive Office of the White House. It was far from being the only tobacco stain on the dark paisley carpet and would go unnoticed when it dried. Still, Douglas grimaced and unconsciously looked over his shoulder, an instinct acquired from marriage to a culturally refined wife who abhorred "lower class habits" like tobacco-spitting.

His wife Adele, a Southern Lady from the North Carolina plantation aristocracy, *had* managed to work some social refinements on him during the months since he was elected President. He now took a bath on most days and combed his hair. She saw to it that his suits were tailored to the standards befitting a President and were freshly laundered and pressed. But she hadn't succeeded entirely. Besides spitting tobacco, he still drank liquor and used colorful language. And he remained a confirmed agnostic unmoved by his wife's devout Catholic faith.

Nor had becoming President improved Douglas' health. His forty-seven years showed in the lines on his face. The churning of his stomach from a hearty appetite followed by consumption of spirits during after-dinner political discussions rarely allowed him a sound night's rest.

Decades of politicking left his body running in a permanent state of exhaustive nervous energy. Like his predecessors in the White House, he had imagined the prestige of the office would have a soothing effect by elevating him above the tiresome political fray. And, like those before him, he discovered upon taking office that being President was nothing at all like he'd anticipated.

Instead of majestically issuing orders to be carried out by his party loyalists in Congress, he discovered that they expected him to become the servant of their ambitions. He remembered how much he had enjoyed tweaking Presidents when he'd been in Congress. The institutional rivalry between the President and Congress was less amusing when he was on the receiving end. And now as President, he was hounded incessantly by every man who was, or pretended to be, a member of his party, who wanted an appointment to a post office, customs house, judgeship, or federal marshal's office.

Nor did he find as many friends in the press as he expected. The Republican-owned papers accused him of "aspiring to become an even more pompous tin pot emperor than Napoleon's bastard grandson." The British press ridiculed his promise to enforce the Monroe Doctrine. "An old-time bit of diplomatic rubbish," they called it. "The English are the great power in the Americas; and no dog of a republic headed by an over-imbibing demagogic President can open its mouth to bark without our good leave."

Even those Democratic-owned papers that editorialized so thunderously for him during the campaign now accused him of "shirking his responsibilities" by leaving the liberation / conquest of Mexico to state militias that were slow to get organized absent a coordinated national effort.

He knew controversy sold more newspapers than quiet congeniality did, so he should not take their criticisms personally. But the constant carping stung. Could not the Congress and the newspaper editors hold their tongues for even a year and then judge him by the results of "Confederate Union, United Expansion?" He understood now why presidents aged so quickly in office and seemed so joyous when leaving it.

And now he had international firebrands to deal with. He was certain that England, France, and Spain would never have issued their *Joint Proclamation on Containment of Slavery* if the Free States had not emboldened them by ratifying the Cleveland Convention's resolutions pledging non-support of his Mexican intervention.

106

Just yesterday the British Ambassador had condescendingly lectured him on why Britain supported Napoleon III's occupation of Mexico. The ambassador said the depredations of Mexico's perpetual civil war were not only an affront to civilization but a threat to global commerce because Mexico's Isthmus of Tehuantepec would soon become the link between the Atlantic and Pacific. The ambassador reiterated his government's opposition to slavery, making it clear that Britain would not tolerate intervention by the Americans in Mexico for the purpose of spreading slavery into the country. It was therefore the duty of Europe, not the slave-owning Americans, to restore Mexico's civil government.

So, Douglas was faced with the most difficult calculation of his political life. His political instinct "told" him that a joint declaration of war by the European powers would unite Americans in all sections in a fury greater than the fury they held against each other. Americans of the Slave States and Free States fighting side-by-side would surely brace a shaky Union just as it had back in 1812.

Even if the war was unsuccessful, the Confederate Union at worst would emerge with its pride ruffled and with perhaps an obligation to pay some nominal reparations. But its territory would remain intact, and its people united and gritting their teeth for a rematch. Of course, Douglas did not intend to be defeated. He, Davis, McClellan, and Secretary of the Navy Caleb Cushing had begun planning for what McClellan called the Transcontinental War.

McClellan's war plan called for the Confederate Union to feint toward Mexico with its state-organized militias, while making another call for volunteers in a National Army to be staged along the Ohio River. After drawing the British and French into Mexico with state militias, the Confederate Union would turn its national armies on the Ohio northward and roll up British North America from Sarnia to Montreal. In the meantime swarms of Confederate commerce raiders would be sweeping the seas clean of British, French, and Spanish merchant ships.

The final phase of McClellan's plan called for the Confederate Union Navy to lay down the keels of ocean-going battleships in the East Coast ports, then sortie into the Caribbean to destroy the combined European fleet. The loss of its ocean-going fleet would render the European Powers' position in the Americas untenable. The national consciousness would be stirred to envisage a future wherein the whole of the Western Hemisphere would be held under the flag of the Confederate Union.

Douglas considered what to do. Should he order the Southern state militias to proceed into Mexico immediately, knowing he would risk provoking war with the European Powers? Or should he wait for the Confederate Union to grow stronger in two or three years after recruiting a large professional army and constructing a modern navy? He had planned to make this the primary topic for today's Cabinet meeting, steering the conversation toward convincing the Cabinet that the time to act was now. He would ask them to authorize the "liberation" of Mexico by the Southern militias now, then see how things sorted out with the Europeans.

It appeared, however, that something was brewing in Indiana that might preempt the preemption he was planning in Mexico. He had received the first inkling of it from Secretary of War McClellan yesterday evening --- something about an armed clash between a party of slave catchers and a posse of Free State men from Michigan and Indiana. This had to be the first order of business at today's Cabinet meeting.

After clearing his mouth of tobacco, Douglas greeted the Cabinet members milling about in the Executive Office. All were present except Caleb Cushing who was away inspecting the Brooklyn Navy Yard and Treasury Secretary Howell Cobb who was meeting with the New York City bankers.

Douglas called them to order, taking his place in a chair at the end of the too-small table while the others crowded their chairs around the table as near as they could get. He called first upon Secretary of War George McClellan, who was holding a sheaf of telegraphed reports from his former business associates in the railroads, and was therefore the most fully informed.

"Mac, what in the name of holy hell is going on in Indiana?"

McClellan looked around at the other Cabinet members to make sure he had everyone's attention. "These reports were telegraphed by Franklin Edson, president of the Louisville, New Albany, and Chicago Railroad. They were reported to him by an engineer who witnessed the events first hand."

"I know Frank," replied Douglas. "He's a reliable man. What does he report?"

McClellan grasped the sheaf of telegrams in both hands and summarized them as he read.

"Mr. Edson's engineer reported a skirmish between a party of slave catchers and Free State men near Delphi, Indiana --- that's halfway between Chicago and Indianapolis --- that started the day before yesterday. The engineer was told the slave party numbering about twenty men had raided the Negro settlements in Cass County, Michigan on Monday morning. They made off with five or six Negroes. However, one of the Negroes got away and alerted the Cass County Sheriff who raised a posse to follow them. On Wednesday afternoon the posse got ahead of the slave party and blocked their route down the Tippecanoe River west of Delphi. The posse stretched a chain across the river. They forced the slave party's boat ashore and have them surrounded. The two parties have been taking potshots at each other since then."

"Anybody hurt?" asked Douglas.

"A couple of Free State men are reported to have been hit by fire from the slave party. One is reported to have died. No report on casualties in the slave party."

McClellan held up another message from his sheaf of telegrams. "This morning Mr. Edson obtained another report from the Chicago stationmaster. The stationmaster reported that Elmer Ellsworth reserved a car for his militiamen yesterday afternoon. At that time the nature of the disturbance in Indiana wasn't clear. Ellsworth's men were allowed to board with their equipment including weapons and ammunition. That's a direct line to Delphi. Ellsworth will be arriving there soon if he hasn't already."

"I knew Ellsworth in Chicago," replied Douglas. "He's a hell of a fine military man, but I don't expect he'll be on our side in this controversy. We need to dissuade him from doing anything rash."

"I know him too," said McClellan. "I had a pleasant chat with him in New York just before the election. I told him that if this administration was elected, we would consider sending him on military missions like the ones I was assigned by Secretary of War Davis during Pierce's Administration. He's an outstanding young man in every sense of the word. I've already sent him a telegram through the Delphi office asking him to return to Chicago. His militia is privately funded and not under our control. Who knows if he received the message or will heed it if he did. I asked Mr. Edson to order his stationmasters to refuse to

109

board anyone else who wants to go to Delphi unless they have proof of residence in the vicinity. The less people we have there trying to inflame the situation, the quicker we will have it under control."

"It was good of you to think of that," acknowledged Douglas. "Let's hope Ellsworth received the telegram and heeds it."

McClellan lifted another telegram. "This one's from Ohio. Frederick Douglass was in Toledo speaking to an Abolitionist Society when word of the slave raid arrived. He left town yesterday. I think it's safe to assume he'll show up in Delphi."

Douglas shook his head. "All we need is for that crazy Nigger to go adding fuel to the fire."

"He's not the only crazy one stirring the pot," McClellan informed him. "This last report is from Alabama. It was originated by one of our officers in transit through Montgomery. He reports: 'William L. Yancey has contacted Southern newspapers. Claims title to Negroes taken to Indiana. Asks Slave State governors to send help to his men in Delphi.'"

Douglas furiously spit the last remnant of his tobacco wad, this time not caring a whit whether it landed on the carpet. "Should've known Yancey was behind this. He's bound and determined to embarrass this administration. He'll never forgive us for quashing him in Charleston." He looked at Jefferson Davis. "Do you want to try to talk some sense into him?"

Davis shrugged. "Bill Yancey keeps his own councils. But I'll be glad to do whatever I can. I can sympathize with his motives in wanting to teach the Abolitionists to comply with the Fugitive Slave Act, but I deplore his methods. They are not the councils of a prudent man."

"Glad we're agreed," declared Douglas. "We can't tolerate contempt for the law, or contempt for this administration, from any quarter. Is that point clear?"

All present nodded a firm assent.

"Then let's send Yancey a telegram asking him to cease and desist," Douglas told Davis. "If that doesn't calm him, you'll have to get down to Alabama for a palaver. Let

Yancey know he's playing with fire. Tell him I'll send the federal marshals to arrest him if he doesn't call off his dogs."

"Yes, Mr. President," replied Davis. *I'm supposed to be leading our militias into Mexico instead of going to Alabama to sweet talk Crazy Bill Yancey.*

Douglas turned to Attorney General Alexander Stephens of Georgia. "Aleck, what's your legal brief of the incident."

Stephens responded with a decisive voice out of character with his frail body of less than a hundred pounds.

"If Yancey has obtained legal title to these Negroes, they must be presumed to be runaways subject to the Fugitive Slave Act. However, it appears that Yancey's men made no attempt to meet the legal requirements of their recovery. They failed to obtain a warrant for the arrest of the Negroes and thereafter to obtain a court order assigning them to the claimant and permitting their removal out of the state. The capture and removal of these Negroes, without court papers, thereby takes on the legal character of kidnapping."

Secretary of State Horatio Seymour, a thoughtful New Yorker, joined the discussion.

"Yancey has nevertheless succeeded in putting this administration to the test. He will claim it was not possible to proceed through the courts because Michigan has personal liberty laws prohibiting enforcement of the Fugitive Slave Act. So it devolves upon us to decide whether to employ the Federal Authority either to return these Negroes to slavery or to prosecute Yancey's men as kidnappers. If we choose the former, we will have the Free States against us. If we choose the latter, we may inflame the Slave States to rally to Yancey's Secession standard."

"That is surely the result he intended," agreed Douglas, his face turning red with anger. "He couldn't break up the Union in Charleston, so now he thinks he can force us to do it for him."

"Our best course, legally and politically, will be to get this case into the federal courts where it belongs," Stephens advised. "Let the judges decide whether these Negroes should be returned to slavery or set free to return to their homes. We'll have to be creative in finding a court to adjudicate the case. The federal judges in Michigan won't hear cases on slave recoveries. They'd set the Negroes free. Maybe there would be a fair hearing in

111

Indiana. The Administration's position should be that we don't care about the outcome, so long as the proceedings are fair."

Douglas nodded. "You are right, Aleck. This has to go through the federal courts to have a legitimate outcome." He folded his hands under his chin and began to think. "Gentlemen, let's see if we can't put some flesh around the bones of Aleck's proposal. First question is: how do we restore order in Indiana? Do we ask Governor Hendricks to call out the Indiana militia, or do we order the Regular Army to intervene straight away?"

"This is a Federal issue," advised Jefferson Davis. "The Regular Army should handle it."

Douglas turned to Horatio Seymour, a former Governor of New York. "What do you think, Horatio?"

"Jeff is right. Send in the Regular Army. Hendricks might err on the side of caution. Most any governor would in these circumstances. This is a Federal issue and needs to be handled by the Federal Authority from start to finish."

"What Regular Army units would you recommend deploying into Indiana?" Douglas asked McClellan.

"General Harney's Department of the West is headquartered at St. Louis. That's about twelve hundred men. There's another three hundred at Newport, Kentucky. Harney's a decisive commander but intelligent enough to assess the situation when he gets there and respond appropriately to it. If we get him moving now, he'll be there by tomorrow afternoon."

Douglas asked his Cabinet: "Is there any reason we shouldn't order Harney's command to Delphi? Their orders will be to reach the scene of the disturbance and interpose themselves between the slave catchers and Abolitionists. They will disarm both groups. They will escort Ellsworth's men to the next train back to Chicago. They will escort the slave catchers and the captive Negroes to the Federal district courthouse at Indianapolis. Both groups are to be incarcerated pending a court hearing to decide their legal status. Are there any objections to this proposal?"

Jefferson Davis thought a moment. "No objection to the plan itself, but it depends on bringing the case to a judge in Indianapolis who will give a fair hearing. I don't know that there is such a judge in that circuit. Why don't we tell Harney to bring the slave party back to St. Louis and hear the case in the federal court there?"

"I don't think that would be wise, Jeff," Stephens answered. "It would make it look like our administration was an accomplice in kidnapping the Negroes and bringing them into a Slave State jurisdiction. There'll be an uprising in the North for sure if a Missouri court orders these Negroes returned to slavery."

"Then we can't let the case go to Missouri," agreed Douglas. "We can't let it go back to Michigan where it will be laughed out of court. That leaves Indiana. The case can be decided there on the simple question of whether the slave catchers have shown proper legal title to claim the Negroes."

Douglas addressed Stephens. "Aleck, I want you on the next train to Indianapolis. When you get there, work with Governor Hendricks to organize a court of federal commissioners to adjudicate this controversy. Draft them from federal marshals we know will judge the case responsibly. Instruct them as follows:

"If Yancey's men produce proof of ownership of these Negroes the court is to issue the documents authorizing their removal from their residences in Michigan and their delivery to Yancey. Harney will escort the slave party and the Negroes to Kentucky.

"If Yancey's men do not have valid titles. the court is to release the Negroes and allow the Abolition party to escort them back to Michigan. If that be the case, they must find Yancey's men guilty of kidnapping. They will give them suspended sentences on condition they never again set foot in the Free States. Harney's men will guarantee Yancey's party safe passage to Kentucky." Douglas looked at the rest of the Cabinet. "Your thoughts gentlemen?"

"It's a decisive plan," Postmaster General Andrew Johnson remarked. "That's what we need. The worst thing we could do is dillydally in indecision. Our dis-Unionist enemies North and South would take it as a signal to advance their schemes."

Douglas addressed Jefferson Davis. "Jeff, we need to get Yancey out of the country before he stirs up any more trouble. Think you can talk him into accepting the ambassadorship to Great Britain? That will give him something genuinely important to do.

113

Tell him the British are offering to broker a deal whereby Spain will agree to sell us Cuba in return for our acknowledging European hegemony in Mexico."

"Are they really proposing to offer us that swap?" asked Davis.

"How should I know? Tell Yancey to get over there and suggest the idea to Britain's foreign minister. See if anything comes of it. I should have thought of sending Yancey to England before, but hell, I can't think of everything. That's why we've got to put all our heads together. We've got to be thinking every day how to get this country calmed down and get the people back to the business of being Americans. Are we all agreed on this course of action?"

Heads nodded.

"Let's get this thing in Indiana quashed so we can get back to the business that the people elected us to do. Confederate Union, United Expansion!"

17

Delphi, Indiana, May 10, 1861

Elmer Ellsworth's Chicago Zouaves

As he detrained in Delphi, Elmer Ellsworth felt destined to live the most glorious day of his life. He saw a radiantly beautiful spring morning, everything green and leafy under a deeply hued blue sky. The warm air rising from the ground mingled with a crisp breeze coming down from Lake Michigan. The boisterous camaraderie of his fellow volunteer militiamen, the Chicago Zouave Cadets, in their gaudy orange-and-purple uniforms, heartened him with joyful purpose.

All through the night, while the train rolled down from Chicago, they had talked about how they were coming to Delphi to rescue the "kidnapped sons and daughters of Michigan" and then "administer a whupping to the behinds of the slave catchers they'll never forget." They talked about how the mere sight of Ellsworth's splendidly equipped militiamen would overawe the Slavers. After their surrender, Ellsworth would apply a ceremonial "kick in the pants" to each and order them to "Return to the Slave Country from whence you came and never again pollute the Free Soil of the North with your infernal presence."

Ellsworth was certain that a humiliating surrender here would break the back of the Slave Power. Free State men would never again have to hear their blustering threats to leave the Union. Perhaps even their enslaved Negroes would take courage and rise against them. Ellsworth saw himself as the instrument chosen by Providence to liberate the slaves and chastise their masters.

Ellsworth was first off the train. His men came swarming out after him, gathering their rifles and ammunition from the baggage car. Many passengers and those waiting at the station cheered. But for all their military ardor, he and his men had never fired a shot in anger. He expected the only firing today would be a victory salute after the surrender of the slave catchers and the liberation of their victims.

Ellsworth might have been influenced to caution had he read McClellan's telegram:

TO ELMER ELLSWORTH ARRIVING DELPHI ON LNAC RR. URGENT. SITUATION EXTREMELY DANGEROUS. PLEASE RETURN CHICAGO. ADMINISTRATION HAS ACTION UNDER ADVISEMENT. SEC OF WAR G MCCLELLAN.

But he didn't see McClellan's telegram, its transmission having been delayed by the mechanical failure of the repeater at Fort Wayne. He therefore rallied his men to action without delay. "Let's go restore freedom to the free!" he shouted.

His men roared their approval. Some onlookers raised their hats in salute. Ellsworth's men fell in, marching over the railroad bridge across the Wabash. They marched past the elevated aqueduct of the Wabash and Erie Canal over the river. Those who hadn't seen it before marveled at the feat of engineering. They marched past the mile and a half of corn fields between the Wabash and the Tippecanoe. They smelled the scent of upturned earth, recently plowed to receive the corn and beans. As they neared the Tippecanoe, they encountered spectators who hoped to be near the battle but safely out of the line of fire.

Ellsworth reached the high ground on the banks of the Tippecanoe and looked out over the river. The Free State men had stretched a chain across the river and wrapped it around the birches on either side. The slavers' flatboat was run aground on the near bank. Ellsworth saw dozens of Free Staters on both sides of the river, but no sign of the slavers. He presumed they were hunkered down in the thick brush between the ridge and the river or were in the pilot house of the boat keeping an eye on their captives. He ordered his men to halt while he went ahead to reconnoiter.

When he reached the Free State picket line, he introduced himself to the man who seemed to be their commander.

"I'm Sheriff Joe Parker of Cass County, Michigan," replied the leader. "I'm out of my jurisdiction, but the sheriff here didn't want to get involved. He said, it's our people, so it's up to us to get 'em, if we want 'em."

Ellsworth shook his head in disgust. "I don't see how any Northern man can shirk his duty to protect free men from being sold back into slavery. I suppose there are still some who don't think kidnapping a free Negro is worth getting riled up over."

"I am honored to make your acquaintance," said Parker, grasping Ellsworth's hand with confidence that he would get more cooperation than from the local sheriff. "I saw your exhibition in Grand Rapids last July; very impressive. Are you here to help us return the Negroes to freedom?"

"I am indeed, sir," said Ellsworth. "May I ask what is the situation here?"

Parker removed his hat and wiped the sweat from his head. The sun was high enough to bring out the first trace of humidity from the river. He grimaced with obvious contempt for the slave catchers as he told the story.

"The slavers raided the Negro settlements in Cass County, Michigan on Monday. They made off with five free Negroes, but one of the Negro women got away and alerted me. I sent riders out to every county seat in western Michigan and northern Indiana to warn folks to be on the lookout."

"A most salutary response," remarked Ellsworth. "It certainly paid off."

"You learn to be prepared for anything if you've been sheriff long enough," Parker answered. "The slavers tried to throw us off their scent by going to Niles where they had a steamer waiting. They used it to cross over into Indiana, but their captives raised a ruckus when they were being moved into wagons for portage to the Tippecanoe. Somebody figured out what was going on and summoned our friends in St. Joseph County. They're the ones who got here ahead of the slavers and blocked the river."

"Thank heavens for that," said Ellsworth. "Can you imagine how obnoxious those slavers would have become if they'd gotten away with this? We'd have had slave raiders invading every inch of Free Soil."

"You're telling me," agreed Parker, wiping the sweat off his neck again. "The slavers think they own this whole damn country. They've got to learn that this is Free Soil. If we let them march in here and kidnap free men right out from under our noses we might as well not have any country left to call our own. Another thing I'm tired of is this 'Confederate Union' Douglas keeps talking about. What's wrong 'The 'United States?' They sound like they're ashamed of the country the way it was and are trying to make it into something else."

"Isn't that the truth? Well, we'd best put a stop to that nonsense right here and now." Ellsworth saw movement and pointed to the brushy river banks. "Is that where the slavers are hiding out?"

"Yes, that's them. They're on our side of the river. One or two are on the boat keeping an eye on the Negroes."

"I don't suppose there's any chance of talking them into surrendering?" Ellsworth asked, suddenly aware that an attack might mean death for some of his men, including him.

"We tried to reason with them," Parker replied. "Day before yesterday we offered them safe passage to Kentucky if they would release the Negroes. Got no response to our parleys except for a volley of gunfire later in the day. Tell the truth, it started with one of the Abolitionists on the other bank who had too much to drink and let off a few pistol shots in the air. The slavers were aiming to kill us when they returned fire. Three of our men were hit and one has died. My deputy's one of the wounded. He's in the doctor's house with a shattered arm he's probably going to lose. I think you can understand why we're not trying to talk to these animals any longer."

Ellsworth stiffened on the news that blood had been spilled. Until now, he'd thought this would be another parade ground exercise. Form the men up, march them forward with bayonets thrusting, and intimidate the slavers into surrendering. In his mind's eye he had seen them surrendering with their heads held down and their arms held high, begging to be released so they could return home and never cause trouble in these parts again. But hearing of yesterday's casualties warned him this would not be a bloodless battle. His gut churned.

"Military protocol dictates that you, being the first to arrive on the site, are in command," Ellsworth acknowledged. "I'm at your disposal. I'd like to propose, however, that we finish this situation now before the slavers figure a way to escape. I propose the following plan of attack: my men will break their line with a coup de main. As soon as we get behind them, your men will attack from the front. Keep your men close enough together to prevent any of the slavers from escaping around you. Some of us and some of your men may get killed. Are your men prepared to pay the price, if it comes to that?"

"We know what we have to do," answered Sheriff Parker. "Those Negroes are free, by God. They are citizens of the State of Michigan and legal residents of Cass County. I have a sworn duty to protect them. Besides they're our friends and neighbors. It's a personal matter of pride for us, as well as a matter of principle. We'll do what our conscience and duty commands."

Ellsworth shook Parker's hand. He felt the weight of responsibility for the life and death of his men. "Please tell your men to be ready to follow us in ten minutes."

He instructed his men: "Fall in to attack column, three abreast! Load your weapons and fix bayonets! Remember to aim carefully when you fire, then charge in quick to finish them off with the bayonet!"

Ellsworth didn't waste time second-guessing his decision. The less time the slavers had to react, the better were his odds of overrunning them with fewest losses. He watched his men prepare their weapons. Some were sweating more profusely than the humidity rising from the river could account for. A few minutes later the thumping of bullets being rammed home and the clinking of bayonets being attached to rifles ceased. He looked over at Parker who was holding his sheriff's revolver. His men had their assortment of weapons ready. Parker nodded.

Ellsworth stepped to the head of his column, marched to the top of the embankment, and held his sword high over his head. "F...o...r...w...a...r...d..........c...h...a...r...g...e...!"

119

Jefferson Buford had twenty men with him down in the brush, hard-bitten veterans of the Mexican War of the late 1840s and the "bleeding Kansas" violence of the late 1850s. He knew the Free Staters, after losing some of their men in the exchange of fire yesterday, would be out for blood.

He hoped the three men he'd assigned to follow the boat on horseback had escaped before the Free Staters sprung their trap the day before yesterday. Hopefully they had reached a telegraph office and alerted Yancey to send help. Perhaps militiamen from all over the South were hurrying to his rescue. Or maybe President Douglas had ordered the Regular Army to intervene. If he could break up this attack it would buy another day's time to wait and see what developed.

He shouted to his men hiding in the brush to hold their positions, aim carefully, and open fire when he did. Ellsworth's column came charging directly at him, shouting "Hurrah!!!!" with Ellsworth in the lead. Buford was armed with a double barreled shotgun loaded with buck and ball. He stood up, leveled it at Ellsworth's chest, and pulled the trigger.

Ellsworth lost consciousness before his senses had time to register the blast tearing through his heart and lungs. The blast also took down his flag-bearer behind him. Buford swung the barrel to the right and pulled the second trigger, blowing a hole in the chest of Ellsworth's second-in-command.

Several slavers stood up and fired a volley from their shotguns and pistols into the tight-packed column, dropping another half dozen men. Ellsworth's remaining men went into a frenzy. Two thrust their bayonets into Buford then stepped back and shot him dead. The Free Staters on the far bank opened up. Their wild firing mostly went high and took down more of Ellsworth's men and Parker's who followed them.

Ellsworth's survivors roared another "Hurrah!" and rushed to the river, wheeling left and right, executing Ellsworth's plan to take the slavers from the rear. Parker's men fanned out in front of the slavers while the Free Staters on the far bank kept up an undisciplined fire, seeming not to care whether they hit friend or foe.

The shooting, clubbing, and bayonetting went on for fifteen minutes as Ellsworth's men and the Free Staters who joined them hunted the slavers in the brush. Ellsworth's men discovered that killing other men who were equally determined to kill them was a grueling business. The slavers, organized by Buford into pairs, shot Ellsworth's men and the Free Staters point blank with pistols and shotguns, knocking down several men with each volley then charging the survivors with bowie knives. In a fury, Ellsworth's men and the Free Staters exterminated the slavers to the last man, finishing them off with bayonet thrusts and pistol shots to the head. Sheriff Parker and his Cass County deputies reached the grounded boat and killed the two slavers guarding the Negroes.

Ellsworth's militia lost twenty-nine of their fifty-five men. Eleven, including Ellsworth, his flag bearer, and his first officer, were dead. A couple of the wounded were in bad shape and not likely to live. Sheriff Parker's posse had four killed and eleven wounded, including three critically.

Sheriff Parker and his Cass County deputies brought the shackled Negroes out of the boat. Eddie Bates held shackled and blindfolded in boats and wagons for four days, and terrified out of his wits, winced at the sunlight, rubbed his aching hands, and involuntarily cried out with joy. "Lord have mercy, Lord have mercy, praise the Lord you got here in time to save us."

"We wouldn't have rested until we rescued you," said Sheriff Parker.

Parker looked over at the dead and wounded men whose blood was trickling into the river. He saw Elmer Ellsworth lying dead on his back, the militia company's crumpled flag lying over him. He took off his hat and pointed their way.

"Those men led the charge to save you. Their commander is...was ...a young fellow from Chicago named Elmer Ellsworth. Some of our Cass County neighbors were killed too, and some are laid up badly wounded."

Eddie had tears running down his face. "God bless your souls! I wondered whether they was anybody who cared about what happened to us!"

"Of course they cared," added Emma who'd come up. "Folks in town was getting' tired of going without their lunches with you not there to run the bakery!"

The men nearby laughed loudly. Even Eddie managed to squeak out a laugh.

"Now, isn't that just like you, Emma, makin' jokes when people is bein' saved from slavery!"

121

The wind blew the stench of blood and feces from the dead bodies into Eddie's face. Hungry and dehydrated, and shaking with nervous exhaustion, he threw up. As a fastidious person, he hated vomiting. This time he barely noticed it. If one looked closely, they would see a tear running down his cheeks, for the first time in years. Part of it might have been his grief over the men who had given their lives to save his, and part of it was his understanding of their love for him that moved their hearts to do it.

18

Delphi, Indiana, May 11, 1861

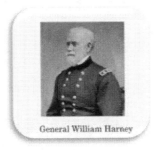

General William Harney

Brigadier General William S. Harney considered himself a tough but fair-minded commander. The Indians out on the Great Plains trusted him to help them fight the outlaws bent on stealing what little was left of their lands. He befriended the Indian warriors and competed fearlessly with them in their ferocious games. He was one of only a handful of Whites the Indians ever welcomed into their councils as a true and respected friend, an equal in courage.

The Indians also knew another side of Harney's nature. Those who had gone on the warpath against him and lived to tell about it called him "the woman killer" because of his propensity to massacre hostiles of all ages and sexes in battle. Harney asked the Indians to respect his authority as the agent of the American government. Those who did became his blood brothers. Those who didn't died.

The men in Harney's command had also experienced the full range of his nature. He had led his men to victory during the Mexican War. However, one of his companies of foreign-born Irish-Catholic men had deserted and joined the Mexican Army. When Harney captured the deserters he executed them without formality of courts martial, including one in the hospital with his legs shot off. Harney had dragged "that legless son of a bitch" out of his hospital bed and strung him up with the rest of the miscreants. In other incidents he had been court-martialed four times for challenging fellow officers to duels and tried in civil court for beating to death a female slave who had lost his house keys.

Like many other Douglas voters, he equally loathed Southern Secessionists and Northern Abolitionists who disturbed the peace of the country. He couldn't care less whether Negroes labored for their own accounts or their masters'. What he did mind were extremists in the North and South who used slavery as a wedge to splinter the Union.

Harney thus arrived at Delphi having neither sympathy nor animosity for either the slavers or the Free State men. If he could defuse the situation by appealing to both parties' reason he would do it. If reason didn't suffice he was prepared to order his men to open fire on either or both parties. He calculated that if violence became necessary he would cooperate with one party to take down the other and then turn his guns on the survivors of the cooperating party. Perhaps he would enjoy hanging some of the wounded, like he had done with that legless turncoat in Mexico. Let the people watch the wounded thrash around at the end of a noose before they died, then see how enthusiastic anybody else was to defy his authority wielded on behalf of his government.

His apprehension that this encounter might turn violent had increased when he detrained in Indianapolis last night and picked up the newspapers. Down in Alabama some idiot named "Yancey" was calling for the mobilization of Southern State militias to invade Indiana and rescue of the besieged slavers. Abolitionist radicals in the North were calling on their Wide Awake paramilitaries to flock to the scene and "extirpate from our free land the vile stain of the slave masters."

After reading the newspapers at Indianapolis, Harney had telegraphed his headquarters command at Jefferson Barracks and ordered two more companies entrained. He ordered the first to detrain at the Indianapolis station and await further orders. He ordered the second to proceed to New Albany, across from Louisville, and secure the Ohio River crossings, including the terminal of the LNAC railroad, in case any more slave raiders thought about crossing the river to come to the aid of their friends at Delphi. He ordered the command at Newport, Kentucky to secure the Ohio River crossings at Cincinnati.

It was in this frame of mind that Harney and one hundred eighty of his men detrained in Delphi. What he saw when he got off the train reminded him of a funeral and a circus. Ellsworth's survivors had wrapped the bodies of their dead in sheets, ready to be placed in the freight car going back to Chicago. The Free Staters had stacked their dead

124

beside their wagons, preparing to return to their homes in Michigan. Somebody had brought in the bodies of a few dead slavers and posed them on the courthouse square where they stood propped up on timbers with flies buzzing around them.

The circus aspect was also apparent. Dozens of newspaper reporters and onlookers were milling around. Vendors were hawking "souvenirs of the battle" including weapons taken from the dead slavers and the chains busted off the Negro captives. A couple farmers were selling barbequed pork from a spit while others sold 'shine from their wagons.

Frederick Douglass had arrived from Toledo. He was giving a rousing speech to cheering Abolitionists on the courthouse steps just clear of the swarms of flies buzzing around the posed bodies of the dead slavers. Harney had never met Douglass but took an instant disliking to him based on the circumstances. *That's all I need, a loud-mouthed Nigger stirring up another heap of trouble.*

Harney interrogated John Barrie, the surviving officer of Ellsworth's command. The extermination of the Slavers and the heavy casualties they had inflicted upon Ellsworth's men and the sheriff's posse warned him that this was still a potentially explosive situation that needed to be tamped down before any more outsiders arrived to inflame it. To establish his authority he began issuing orders, as he had learned to do in occupied towns during the Mexican War.

He ordered two of his men to secure the telegraph office and prevent the transmission or receipt of telegrams to anyone other than himself. He ordered the train station secured to prevent the detraining of anyone without proof of residence in the vicinity. He ordered a squad to conscript some of the bystanders and put them to work interring the dead Slavers outside of town. As he had hoped, the prospect of conscripted labor began dispersing the other bystanders back to their homes. He asked Ellsworth's survivors to return to Chicago with their dead, except for John Barrie who asked to remain behind to see to the proper care of the wounded.

He confronted Sheriff Parker and the lackadaisical local sheriff.

"I am in authority here, by order of the President."

"Yes, Sir!" shouted the local sheriff, relieved to have responsibility lifted from his shoulders.

Harney addressed Sheriff Parker. "Let me know if my command can be of assistance in expediting your return home. I would like for you to be on your way as soon as possible. You may leave one of your men here to look after the welfare of your wounded."

"Most of our people will head home tomorrow morning," Parker replied. "The doctor says the Negroes need another couple days' rest before they're fit to go back home, so a few of us will stay behind to look after them. The slavers didn't feed them anything more than a couple handfuls of parched corn and scarcely gave them any water."

"The Negroes will not be going home with you," declared Harney. "My orders are to escort them to the Federal Court in Indianapolis."

"I've lost five Cass County men killed," Parker replied sternly. "There's three more lying gutshot in the doctor's house who may not make it. Are you telling me I have to surrender the Negroes my men died saving so that Douglas can make them slaves? General, these are *free* men and women. They are citizens of the State of Michigan. They're my friends and neighbors. It is my sworn duty to protect them, and that I will do."

"Sheriff, you did your duty to your people, same as I would have were I in your shoes," Harney said, meaning every word. "But I have my orders directly from the President to deliver these Negroes to the Federal Court in Indianapolis that will lawfully decide their fate. It's about more than these Negroes. It concerns the whole country."

The lines in Parker's face tightened. "You know it's a foregone conclusion that any court convened by the Douglas Administration is going to order these Negroes returned to slavery. Can't you 'look the other way' for an hour while I get them out of here. The slavers are all dead, so who is there left to complain?"

"General Harney, we've lost eleven of our men killed," added John Barrie. "Another couple aren't likely to make it out of here alive. There'll be hell to pay in Chicago if the Negroes are returned to slavery. Sheriff Parker's got a point. Nobody's going to blame you if the Negroes happen to disappear from here and turn up safe at home."

Frederick Douglass joined the group with all his imposing presence. Harney grimaced. *Here's the loudmouth coming to make trouble.* He expected Douglass to harangue the group with high-sounding Abolitionist platitudes about the Negroes' "God-given rights to be free."

126

Instead Douglass addressed him in a soft-spoken voice barely above a whisper. "General Harney, I just spoke to one of the captive Negroes whom these brave men gave their lives to return to freedom. His name is Eddie Bates. He is thirty-seven years of age. He's been living free since his father brought him North as a young boy. General, will you be the instrument that tears Eddie Bates away from his wife and home, robbing him of the life of a free man he has known for almost all his life?"

Douglass turned toward the station where Ellsworth's survivors were loading their dead into the baggage car. "Those men gave their lives to save Eddie and his neighbors from being returned to a fate worse than death. Can you and your command not do as Sheriff Parker suggests, and turn your heads for a little while? I most humbly implore you to listen to the mercy God placed in your good heart and allow the free Negroes to go home. Let this incident end, where it began, with those people back in their homes and living in the freedom that the God who watches over all of us has blessed them with."

Harney was moved by Douglass' gentle words. The slavers *were* dead. Nobody around here would care if the Negroes "disappeared" and were never heard of again. And Frederick Douglass was persuasive because he was right, by damn. If Harney did "look the other way" perhaps the Negroes would go home unobserved and the incident would begin to lose steam.

However, the newspaper reports he'd read in Indianapolis made him aware that the event had already spread beyond Indiana. He had to assume that the Douglas Administration had a larger view of the situation than he did. He therefore decided he must execute his orders to the letter.

"This is the hardest duty I have had to do in my many years of service to my country," Harney explained. "But it *must* be done. The Negroes *will* accompany my command to Indianapolis and *will* be released to the authority of the Federal Court. Mr. Douglass, if you desire to make a plea on their behalf, it will have to be made there."

Frederick Douglass again spoke softly. "General, will you do the free Negroes a courtesy before you take them away? Will you go with me and talk to Eddie Bates and tell him face-to-face that he's going back to slavery? Will you tell him he's never going to see his wife, his neighbors, or his home again? Will you tell him he's never going to take another breath of air as a free man for the rest of his days. Will you tell him that and then decide if your duty compels you to deliver him and the other Negroes to the slave court that will bind them in chains?"

Harney was not inclined toward explaining his orders. But Douglass' demeanor commanded his respect.

"Mr. Douglass, I would accommodate the Negroes if this issue involved only us. But it has already become a national issue. The southern agitator who set up this raid is asking President Douglas to call out the Southern state militias. The Abolitionists and Wide Awakes are sending their men here. My orders are to get these Negroes to Federal Court where their case can be legally processed before this situation explodes and blows the nation apart. I can't be responsible for unleashing a civil war by disobeying my President's orders."

Douglass' demeanor stiffened. "Maybe we **should** have a civil war, if that is what it takes to right the wrong of free men and women being returned to bondage! Our grandfathers fought a war to liberate this country from a king who made not a single one of them his slave. And now the day has come when free men are killing free men to deliver free men into slavery!"

Harney became enraged, all the more so because Douglass spoke with righteous conviction. "That's enough! I'm going to get those Negroes. Anyone who resists will do so at peril to their lives!"

Parker stood firm. "General, if you want to take these Negroes it will have to be over the dead bodies of me and my men."

Fred Douglass stood next to Parker. "Thank you, Sheriff."

John Barrie also stood his ground. "My men aren't leaving here until the Negroes are returned to freedom."

Harney was enraged to fury. "I am declaring martial law in this county. There will be no further warnings!" He shouted to his men, "Let's go get those Negroes. Any man who stands in your way gets the bayonet!"

Harney marched forward. John Barrie, blocking his way, started to move backward. Parker stood firm. Harney called to his soldiers, "Place that man under arrest!"

Those present would remember this as one of those pivotal moments of history, of which revolutions are born, when the laws of men conflicted irreconcilably with their consciences.

An ancient man with shock-white hair and a lean, wind-burned face stepped slowly forward from the crowd and confronted Harney. Everybody in Delphi seemed to know the man, but no one could name him. Some said he looked like the old Unitarian Pastor who used to ride in from Logansport. Some swore he was the itinerant schoolteacher who had roamed the backwoods townships and taught them "by littles" when they were children. Some claimed he'd been the militia colonel who fought with General Harrison at Tippecanoe in 1813.

Whoever he was, the ancient stranger walked right up in front of Harney and planted his carved hickory cane firmly in the ground. He looked Harney straight in the eye and spoke in the confident voice of command.

"Halt!"

The word thundered from ancient lips and echoed across the town square. ***"This is Free Soil. It is free by the Blessing of God and by the Ordinance of Man. You shall not trespass another step upon it."***

Harney kept moving until he was eyeball to eyeball with the old man. Then he stopped. The soldiers marching behind him also stopped in their tracks.

John Barrie, inching away from confrontation, came back and stood firm at the old man's side. Barrie looked Harney in the eye. "Declare martial law, you say? Indeed, General, you'd best read the Constitution. Only Congress can declare martial law!"

Frederick Douglass stepped forward to close the gap on Barrie's left. The townspeople milling about took courage. They too closed ranks and interposed themselves between Harney's men and the doctor's house sheltering the recovering Negroes.

The ancient stranger spoke to the people, in a booming voice that carried across the square, "Stand firm! Free Soil men are coming. They will help us!"

Harney considered ordering his men to break the line. The look of steadfast determination on his opponents, some of whom were armed, told him it would take a rifle volley followed by a bayonet charge. He looked the white-haired stranger in the eye and

129

blew hot breath in his face. The old man moved not a muscle. Harney hesitated. These people were not going to back down. Stories of Lexington, Concord, and the Boston Massacre came to mind. Firing on them might touch off an armed revolt by every Free Soil man within a hundred miles, maybe throughout the whole North. He decided to stand firm and wait it out. His Regular Army men, trained to hold their place in line for hours, could wait until the civilians dispersed from hunger, thirst, fatigue, and boredom. He did not think it would take longer than an hour for them to begin heading back to their homes.

Ten minutes passed, then twenty, then an hour, then an hour and a half. The ancient stranger kept his place. Beside him unmoving stood Sheriff Parker, John Barrie, and Frederick Douglass. The citizens held firm behind them. Harney fumed in silence. Two hours passed. *The old geezer will have to go take a leak sometime. I can wait him out.*

Then Harney noticed a cloud of dust rising up out of the east. Five minutes later he heard the sound of drumming. A man from the edge of town came running up. "The Wide Awakes are here! Thousands of them! From Detroit, Fort Wayne, South Bend, and Toledo!" Harney watched them come marching into town in perfect order, their drummers leading the way. They were young, healthy men. And they were singing a new song in rhythm with their drums, a song honoring the martyr who had given up his life in an ill-planned quest to liberate the slaves:

> *John Brown's body lies a-mouldering in the grave,*
> *But His soul's still marching on.*
> *He's gone to be a soldier in the army of the Lord,*
> *His soul's a-marching on.*
> *Hurrraaaaaaaaaaaaaaaaaaaahhhhhhhhhhhhhhhhhh!!!!!!!!!!!!!!!!!!!!!!!!!!!!!!!*

Many held the torches which were standard issue for Wide Awakes, but some carried firearms. Each Wide Awake club flew a different flag. The leading banner appeared to have been designed for last year's election with Lincoln's name, a gold star, and an eye flanked by a couple weasels:

In front of the banner came a man who seemed in command. He moved forward and entered the line next to the ancient stranger.

He addressed General Harney: "I am Jacob Loomis, Commanding Officer of the Ohio Division of the Army of the Republic of Free America! The Negroes are coming with us. *You* are to vacate the premises, and I mean *now*."

19

The White House, May 13, 1861

President Stephen Douglas rolled up his sleeves and unbuttoned his shirt collar, as if to make clear to his Cabinet that the time for heavy labor in service to the country had come. He had a leaf of paper and a pen handy. He did not often take notes at Cabinet meetings but this time he wanted to be sure nothing of substance slipped his memory.

A fresh breeze from the open window caught his collar, drying the sweat from his neck. He turned his head toward the tall window. The cool winds and sunny skies blowing across Indiana had arrived in Washington City, clearing the early spring humidity from the air. The breeze and its scent of budding vegetation recalled memories of a young man on the outdoor stump on the Illinois prairie a quarter-century ago.

He smiled inwardly at those happy memories of the joys and triumphs of his life. He had come out to Illinois at twenty-two, an unknown bumpkin from Vermont. Five years later he sat on the Illinois Supreme Court, the youngest person ever to hold that position. He had gone on to Washington as a Congressman and then a Senator, his name etched in the national memory of the great political debates over slavery, transcontinental railroads, and western homesteads.

It had taken longer than expected to accustom himself to the role of Chief Executive of the nation. Instead of making frilly speeches in Congress urging the president to take actions he favored, he *was* the president, deciding the course of momentous events that would echo down the generations. Having a deep-rooted instinct for wielding political power, he understood he must take control of all issues coming under his purview, and shape them his way, before they took control of him. He therefore called the Cabinet Meeting to order with a tone of confident authority. He turned again to McClellan to make the opening statement.

"Mac, please bring us up to date on events transpiring in Indiana."

McClellan sat behind the usual stack of War Department telegrams. "Mr. President, I will read from the telegrams sent by General Harney from Delphi:

"On the afternoon of May 11 General Harney detrained at Delphi with two companies totaling 180 men. He reports that on the day previous, Ellsworth's men, reinforced by Michigan and Indiana Abolitionists, assaulted the slave party they had run aground on the Tippecanoe River near its juncture with the Wabash. They succeeded in liberating the Negroes held captive after killing the entire slave party of twenty-one men."

That got the Cabinet's attention. They sat bolt upright and looked at McClellan incredulously.

"It was a battle to the death!" exclaimed Horatio Seymour.

"It was for the slave party," replied McClellan. "Ellsworth's militia company also suffered severely. Twenty-nine of their fifty-five men were shot. Thirteen were killed outright or have since died of their wounds." A mist appeared in McClellan's eye and his voice cracked. "I, I very much regret to say that Elmer Ellsworth was killed while leading the assault." He composed himself. "The Abolitionists from Michigan and Indiana also lost five men killed and a dozen wounded. Some of their wounded aren't expected to live."

"Damn," said Douglas, slamming down his pen. "Ellsworth was an excellent young man and a good American. I am very much afraid his death will make him a martyr among the Republicans. It will inflame them to opposition against this government as few other things would have."

"I regret to report it already has," McClellan informed him. "I have a report concerning the deaths of three slavers who left the main body the day their boat was run aground. They're the ones who reached the telegraph office at Lafayette and got off the telegram to Yancey. They were captured by Abolitionists yesterday evening. After learning of Ellsworth's death, the Abolitionists summarily executed them."

Douglas shook his head and slammed down his fist again. "Damn it to hell! That is going to incite the slave holders to a wrathful vengeance. What's going on in Delphi now?"

McClellan shuffled his stack of telegrams. "The last report from Harney is that he is engaged in a standoff with the Free State men. Harney's men control of the railroad station and telegraph office. The Free State men are blocking their entry to the doctor's house where the Negroes are recovering. The survivors of Ellsworth's company remain in Delphi in defiance of Harney's orders. The posse from Michigan also refused Harney's orders to leave town and is being reinforced by Wide Awake organizations from surrounding counties in Indiana, Michigan, and Ohio. Frederick Douglass is there too and is no doubt adding fuel to the fire."

Postmaster General Andrew Johnson showed a look of utter disgust. "You should order Harney to shoot that mischievous old goat straight away. That'd be the one happy outcome of this fiasco."

Douglas rolled his eyes. He **would** have ordered Harney to shoot Fred Douglass in a heartbeat if he thought Douglass' demise would tamp down the situation. But the last thing the country needed right now was another martyr. Douglas motioned for McClellan to continue.

"Harney ordered another company to Indianapolis and another one to New Albany. I presume he intends to use the men in Indianapolis to guard the slave court proceedings. He has ordered the men in New Albany to secure the Ohio River crossings against militias from the Slave States trying to make their way to Delphi. I've released the men at Newport Barracks across from Cincinnati to his authority. They're guarding the Ohio River crossings in that vicinity."

"Do we have any reports of Slave State militia men trying to enter Indiana?" Douglas asked.

"No reports of anything like that so far," McClellan answered. "But we have reports of trouble in the Northwest."

"Where?"

"Clashes are reported between Wide Awakes and our United Invincibles in Illinois at Joliet and Springfield. At Joliet some Wide Awakes were attempting to load an old courthouse cannon into a train bound for Delphi via Chicago. Their neighbors dumped the cannon into the Des Plaines River. At Springfield one of our Invincibles shot and killed a Wide Awake in a barroom brawl. Mr. Lincoln happened to be making a speech at the Illinois State Fairgrounds. Lincoln's crowd rushed into town when they heard about the barroom shootout. No word yet if anybody else has been hurt."

"You can always count on somebody getting shot in the Springfield bars," said Douglas. "There's a lot of riff-raff in that town. Most of them are our voters!" Despite being a well-heeled state capital, Springfield, like every other western town, had more than its share of roughnecks.

"There's also a spat going on in Detroit between some Irishmen and Republicans in the downtown bars," continued McClellan. "Only insults and fisticuffs so far, but where the Irish are involved, anything can happen."

"Isn't that the truth!" agreed Douglas. "At least the Irish will be on our side if we have to call out the militia to restore order in the Abolitionist cities."

"The Irish saved our necks in a couple of campaigns in New York City," remarked Seymour. "They're good people to have on your side, whether it's in a political campaign or around a bar."

McClellan read deeper into the sheaf of telegrams. "This one arrived less than an hour ago. It reports unrest in and around St. Louis. The Missouri State Militia got into a shouting match with German Wide Awakes in the city center. With Harney gone to Indiana, the Jefferson Barracks are commanded by Captain Nathaniel Lyon. He's an Abolitionist fanatic, and crazy as a loon from what I've heard. One of the lieutenants reported he's demanding that Governor Claiborne Jackson withdraw his militiamen twenty miles outside St. Louis."

"Relieve Lyon of command at once and have him report here to me," Douglas ordered. "Have men ready to place him under arrest if he refuses. The last thing we need is for the Abolitionists in the military to get in league with their bummers in the government. That would be a recipe for treason."

"Do you think they'd try to organize themselves into a separate government?" asked Seymour incredulously.

"They're capable of it," replied Douglas.

"They're perfectly capable of appealing to the British for protection, too," added Jefferson Davis.

"Do you think the British would negotiate with them?" Seymour asked. "It would involve them in a war with this government if they do."

"We don't have any idea what the Redcoats might do," answered Douglas. "Can't deny that there are a lot of people in New England who would prefer a union with Britain to a union with Slave States. Britain would jump at the chance to provide the Canadas with direct access to the sea through Boston. We have to anticipate there'll be collusion between them and our Free State Abolitionists."

"Let New England go, then," suggested Davis. "Let them go back to the British Empire if that's what they want. Let Upstate New York go too. Let all the Abolitionist country around the Great Lakes go if they want. Why *not* divide the country? There's enough land on this continent for all of us. Better to divide it than to fight over it."

"Oh, no, Jeff, you're wrong about that!" interjected Andrew Johnson in dismay. "We shouldn't give up any territory to the British. We should be trying to get them off of our continent. They'd like nothing more than to divide and conquer us."

Douglas leaned forward. "Andy's right. Even in New England we won forty percent of the votes. We don't have any right to abandon those people to another sovereignty. The Confederate Union is sovereign over every inch of our territory, now and for all time!"

Davis fidgeted. "We at the South hold the view that the states are the people's sovereign instruments of government. I don't think I'd like being told that Mississippi had to remain in the Union contrary to the wishes of her people. I would be inclined to go to war to vindicate Mississippi's sovereignty."

Johnson leaned forward too and looked Davis in the eye. "Jeff, you know that nobody is more loyal to the South than us Tennessee Volunteers. No President did more for the South than 'Old Hickory.' I don't need to tell you about how Andy Jackson felt towards Nullifiers and Dis-unionists! And don't forget how Jefferson and Madison warned the New

136

England Federalists of 'hanging and confiscation' if they didn't cease their defiance of the National Authority prior to and during the War of 1812. No, Jeff, this talk of secession is no part of our Southern tradition."

Douglas became animated. "Secession isn't part of *any* American's tradition! The Republicans and Abolitionists have deluded themselves into thinking they *own* the Free States and can do with them whatever they please, including setting them up as their own country! Well, I've got news for them: the Free State cities are booming with workingmen who vote for us. It won't be long before our voters will be the majority in the Free States. So don't let the Republicans tell you that everybody in the Free States is an Abolitionist who wants to leave the Confederate Union. They're our states as much as theirs."

"If we hold the nation together now, the Abolitionists will disgrace themselves with treason," commented Alexander Stephens. "The people will abandon them, like they abandoned the treasonous, British-loving New England Federalists, while James Madison was fighting the 1812 War."

Davis was intrigued. "That would augur well for maintaining the Confederate Union under our Democratic administration, wouldn't it? Not just now but for all future generations."

Douglas slammed down his fist, startling them all: "Yes! That's exactly it, Jeff! We have got to hold this country together *now*. If we do, it'll leave the door wide open for our party to recover its strength in the North. Can you imagine how strong we'll be with the Slave State vote in the South and the workingman's vote in the North?" Douglas showed the beatific smile of a ward heeler passing out pre-marked ballots and silver dollars on Election Day.

"Then we'd best prepare to suppress a full-blown insurrection in the Free States if it comes to that," Davis warned. "Maybe this will peter out, but let's make our preparations in case it doesn't."

"Damn right!" shouted Douglas. He noticed McClellan and Andy Johnson nodding in stern agreement. Even mild-mannered Horatio Seymour looked determined. Douglas rapped his thumbs on the table. He reached behind him and picked up the coat he'd thrown over the mantle. He pulled a flask of whiskey out of the inside pocket, swigged it, then looked at McClellan.

"Mac, find out what other Regular Army units we can post to Indiana. And we'd best advise the Southern Governors that orders to assemble their militias in New Orleans are hereby revoked. Tell them to hold in place at the state capitals until we find out if they'll be needed to restore order in the Abolitionist States *before* they set off to liberate the Mexicans."

20

Baton Rouge, Louisiana, May 23, 1861

Robert E. Lee

Robert E. Lee knocked, then stepped through the open door into Superintendent William Tecumseh Sherman's office at the Louisiana Military Academy in Baton Rouge.

"I am Robert E. Lee," he said extending his hand in greeting. "Braxton Bragg, Dick Taylor, and Governor Moore have asked me on call on you, if you would be agreeable to receiving me."

"I am pleased to make your acquaintance, Marse' Robert!" said Cump, using the affectionately respectful salutation men who knew Lee well were prone to using. Sherman had never met Lee, their paths not having crossed during decades of Army service. But Sherman felt he knew Lee well enough by reputation to greet him in that familiar manner. "This is an honor as overdue as it is unexpected."

"The honor is entirely mine," replied Lee. "Your reputation in the Army and now as Superintendent of this Academy commends you. That is why I have been asked to talk to you, providing you will have no reluctance in speaking about your views on the insurrection spreading through the North. I will understand if you wish to keep your thoughts private."

Cump opened his palms as if to show he had nothing to hide. "I will be pleased to discuss my views with you. My opinions on the situation are no secret."

They sat down.

"I am on my way to Washington City to be commissioned General of the Armies of the Confederate Union," Lee explained. "General Scott has retired. I am to take his place."

"My heartfelt congratulations," replied Sherman. "Douglas has chosen wisely. I highly respect General Scott, but no man can be expected to stay in that post forever. Douglas was wise to make this change at the outset of his administration."

Lee smiled. "Thank you, sir. I have come to discuss with you your possible role in restoring the National Authority to the disaffected states. I understand Governor Moore has offered you command of the Louisiana State Militia. The Governor tells me you have declined his offer, preferring instead to return to Ohio and accept command of its militia, now being trained to fight to establish a separate national sovereignty."

Cump laughed. "Well, I must tell you that this rumor of my being offered command of the Ohio Free State Militia is a complete fabrication. Even if it were tendered, I could not at this moment decide whether to accept it. Before deciding on any course I must return to Ohio and get a view of the situation there first hand. I owe it to my family to discuss the situation with them before deciding on my course. To tell you the truth, I am much more inclined to stay out of it than to become an active participant for either side. I am thinking of returning to San Francisco and opening a law office."

"Yes," acknowledged Lee, "I fully understand. If Virginia had found itself to be in such a state of disaffection against the general government, it would vex me terribly to have to decide whether to draw my sword to vindicate its sovereignty. My father had to make that decision when he accepted Washington's commission to suppress the Whiskey Rebellion. His Anti-Federalist friends never forgave him for suppressing what they believed was a justified refusal to pay an unconstitutional tax. They withdrew his credit, forcing him into debtors' prison. He was beaten nearly to death by an Anti-Federalist mob in Baltimore. The setting of friend against friend can never have a satisfactory outcome, not even for the side that prevails."

Sherman leaned back. "You know, I've been thinking about that too. Acts of bad faith from too many people on both sides of the Ohio have heated this country to the boiling point. Every time things start to settle down there's a John Brown or a Bill Yancey come along to stir them up again. I love this country, but maybe it's inevitable that we divide it. I don't know. Maybe my mind will become clear on the subject when I go to Ohio. I will advise you of my decision as soon as it is made."

Lee smiled again in understanding. "I know it would not be productive of me to try to influence your decision. But if your conscience should lead you into placing your loyalty with the National Government, then I am prepared to offer you a command in the forces tasked with restoring the National Authority to Ohio. I believe the rebellion would collapse in Ohio at the mere sight of your command, just as the Whiskey Rebellion disbanded when my father arrived in Pennsylvania. Whatever you may decide, my prayers go with you."

"General Lee, thank you for your counsel. I will carry your words in my heart when I go to Ohio." Sherman walked Lee outside to his waiting coach, congratulating him again and wishing him well in his endeavors. Sherman returned to his office and closed the door. Lee's visit had persuaded him of only one thing --- that he would **not** be going to San Francisco to avoid taking sides in the war. Lee had sought him out because his military reputation destined him to take part in this war. For which side he would figure out later.

21

Springfield, Illinois, June 1, 1861

Abraham Lincoln waited for his son Robert, returning from prep school at Exeter, New Hampshire, to detrain at the Springfield railroad station. Mr. Lincoln had arrived in a melancholy mood deepened by the late afternoon wind blowing occasional rain showers from a dismal overcast sky. His spirits lifted when he saw the magnificent new incarnation of the Free State Flag flying over the station.

Like everything else in the Republic of Free America, the early versions of the flag had been put together in a slapdash manner. Many rival variants had proliferated, none particularly inspiring. This latest incarnation was bold and strikingly beautiful with its dark blue canton expanded to cover the entire left half of the flag and the big gold star centered on the blue with nineteen white stars for each of the Free States surrounding it. Provisional President Fremont had designed it. Fremont was absurdly pompous, but the man did have *style*! And Lincoln knew all too well that style, as well as substance, was vital to successfully launching a new nation.

Lincoln especially liked the new flag because the gold confirmed there was a *national* government at the center, surrounded by state governments on the periphery.

The Confederate Union also had a new flag. It was said to have been designed by the Superintendent of West Point, a Louisiana officer named Beauregard, who wanted a battle flag to distinguish his men from the Free Staters trying to take West Point away from its Confederate Union garrison.

The new Confederate Union flag retained the 33-starred canton of the old "Stars and Stripes" making clear that it claimed sovereignty over all the states, Free and Slave. It replaced the horizontal stripes with a white background and red bar. The white was said to symbolize the race of English ancestry while the red, a tad lighter than the dark red of the United States flag, symbolized the French ancestry of Louisiana.

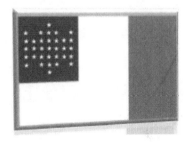

It represented the Confederate Union as a new nation coextensive with the old United States. Lincoln suspected that the old "Stars and Stripes" had fallen as much out of favor in Confederate Union territory as it had here.

He noted that the two flags hinted at many territorial disputes sure to come: Kansas was included as a State in the nineteen stars of the Free State flag but was still an un-starred Territory of the Confederate Union. If the Free States won their independence, there was sure to be haggling over which of the Western Territories they acquired. For that matter there would be haggling over how much of Indiana, Illinois, New York, New Jersey, and Pennsylvania they were awarded, those states being only partially inside the Free States' military frontier. Lincoln had the oddly funny notion that before all was said and done, there might be some half-stars, quarter-stars, and even eighth-stars in both flags!

The Free States would have to vindicate their independence on the battlefield before negotiating for a border. If the Confederate Union prevailed, the number of stars in the Free State flag wouldn't mean anything to anybody other than history students.

It took much longer than usual for the passengers to detrain, as each was questioned by men wearing the Free State Gold Star on their dark blue armbands. Lincoln supposed it would not be long before the provisional government began issuing passports to control the movement of people within its frontiers. Everyone would be required to swear loyalty to the Free State Republic and receive a passport or else remove themselves beyond the military frontier.

The "soldiers" patrolling this station were the survivors of Ellsworth's Chicago Militia Company who fought the first battle of the War of Free State Independence. Lincoln knew some of them. John Barrie had been appointed Provost Marshall of the Free State Military District of Springfield, superseding the defunct civil authority. Lincoln's friend Richard Yates would be arriving from Chicago tomorrow or the next day to begin restoring civil authority as the Provisional Governor of the Free State of Illinois. The elected Democratic Governor James Allen had established the seat of government of the Confederate State of Illinois at the former state capital of Vandalia, 75 miles south.

After fifteen minutes of waiting, Lincoln saw his son step on to the station platform. Robert answered the perfunctory questions of the Free State men while Lincoln stepped forward and met him with a formal embrace. "Glad to have you back with us, Son."

Robert embraced his father with equal formality. "I'm glad to be home. I was so worried about Mother and the children when news of the battles in Illinois reached the East." If Mr. Lincoln was annoyed by Robert's omission of him in his worries, he did not show it.

The two said nothing else as they walked toward Mr. Lincoln's carriage. They had more the rivalry of brothers than a relation of father and son. Perhaps the men were as close as they *could* be, Robert having inherited the passionate "Todd" character of his mother, so contrary to his reserved father.

As they rode to the Lincoln's home, Robert gawked at the destruction. Partisan fighting had swept through Springfield a week ago when the Free State Republican Army of Illinois, commanded by U.S. Grant, had come down from Chicago to push John

144

"Blackjack" Logan's Confederate Unionists out of town. A third of the town was destroyed, the ashes of ruined homes and businesses washing out into the streets with the heavy rain. Robert noticed what appeared to be faded bloodstains on the streets. Perhaps the rain would wash those away too.

"Did the Confederates do this?" Robert asked in dismay.

"I don't know that it was done by any under Logan's command," his father answered. "So far as I know, Logan's men didn't molest civilians or destroy property; after all, citizens loyal to their side were as much in danger as ours. Logan's men were party to a 24-hour truce we asked for when things got out of hand. They helped our men fight the fires and restore order. During the truce they evacuated the Capitol and turned the government buildings and their records over to us undamaged."

Lincoln steered the horses around a corner containing the ruins of a burned-out shell of what had been an upper-class boarding house.

"The arson, robberies, and murders were committed by freelance bandits who went back and forth between the lines. I would never have believed such men lived in these parts, but all too many become animals when the laws can't be enforced. We also erred in failing to destroy the liquor in the taverns. Stolen whiskey incited the criminal element fearfully. We executed the bandits we found drunk the next morning, but most melted away when the Confederates withdrew from town.

"How many were killed here?"

"The undertakers reported the burial of a few over three hundred --- Free State Republicans, Confederate Unionists, bandits, and unarmed citizens. A couple hundred more are laid up injured in their homes or in makeshift hospitals on the fairgrounds." Lincoln's voice cracked. "I'm very sorry to tell you that your Aunt Frannie and Uncle Ed died when their home burned down around them. Ed's gun was found near the bodies, so they may have been murdered by the raiders before they torched the house."

Mr. Lincoln wept quietly as the ruins recalled the fury of barbarism that had descended on the peaceable town. Hatred, fear, and notions of revenge had replaced the neighborly atmosphere of a formerly prosperous town. The town was strangely empty, because surviving Confederate Union loyalists, who had made up a little more than half the prewar population, had left town.

If what had happened here had happened in the hundreds of other contested towns, then the deaths might already be in the thousands. Fearful refugees fleeing their homes might be in the hundreds of thousands. Lincoln winced.

This senseless violence must end quickly, before the damage, loss of life, and enmity of civil war degrades us beyond our ability to restore peace.

When their home came into view, Robert saw a crudely sown variant of the Free State Flag flew flapping on a pole next to the carriage house. This was one of the early cluttered versions where the old Stars and Stripes had been augmented by a vertical blue bar sown down the center, with a crudely cut gold star patched on top of that. It seemed to say, "Here's the patched up old flag of a decrepit country." Fremont's flag proclaimed: "Here is the flag of a proud new Republic, created by perfecting the principles of the flawed one it replaced."

"Are we getting close to relieving our men holding St. Louis?" Robert asked while his father unhitched the horses inside the carriage house.

Lincoln shook his head. "Sam Grant's Free State Army never got anywhere near St. Louis. There were too many Douglas men fighting under Logan's command. Grant fought an unsuccessful battle at Carlinville, then decided to fall back and anchor our line here. It runs from Quincy on the Mississippi, along the railroad to Danville, then doglegs down the east bank of the river to Terre Haute, and from there to Indianapolis."

"What about St. Louis?"

"We're not getting enough support in Missouri to count on holding it. Only a few thousand, mostly of German stock, are fighting with Nathaniel Lyon. They're being attacked by Logan's men from the east and north, and by Governor Claiborne Jackson's Confederate Union militias from the Missouri side. They're being supplied by boats we're sending down the Mississippi, but, barring a miracle, the city will fall. The longer they hold out, the more time Grant has to fortify his line through Illinois. It's a strong line anchored by the Toledo and Great Western Railroad. He has invited me to inspect the fortifications he's building to secure it. I'll take you with me to see them tomorrow or the next day."

Lincoln had been too preoccupied with the war in Illinois to think much about the rest of the country. With the railroads and telegraphs disrupted, there was only a trickle of news into Springfield.

"Has there been any of this partisan warfare in the East?" he asked Robert after they put the horses in their stalls. "The telegraph to Chicago wasn't restored until yesterday, so we've had scant news as yet from outside of Illinois."

Robert answered with enthusiasm in discussing the military situation. "The fighting was severe around New York City and Philadelphia, but it's simmered down. There's even some trade between the lines, although both governments tax it coming and going."

Mr. Lincoln smiled. Governments wasted no time in levying taxes. He could imagine customs posts had come up the instant the lines stabilized.

"Where are the lines now?" he asked.

Robert took a towel from his travel bag and wiped the water from his face and neck.

"The Confederate Union lines around Metropolitan New York run from the Hudson Valley a couple dozen miles north of town in an arc going down about midway through New Jersey. Fremont has ordered the construction of defenses to keep the Douglas men from advancing any further north or west. Otherwise they'll break the railroad into Philadelphia and the one across lower New York State. These lines are overloaded due to the loss of terminals in New York and Newark. You have to purchase tickets for civilian travel ten days in advance. I decided to go up through Montreal then across Canada West to Detroit. These days more Americans are travelling that line than Canadians."

"That's a clever way to get here," acknowledged Mr. Lincoln, impressed by his son's resourcefulness. "The Canadas are our backdoor route to New England. We must be sure to maintain good relations with Old England."

"Yes," agreed Robert. "The British and Canadians I met up there think we did the right thing. 'How could you remain part of a Union that legalizes the ownership of human beings?' they said. They are very much our friends."

"That's good," Mr. Lincoln replied. "We will need all the friends we can make. What else is happening in the East?"

"There's been heavy fighting in the coal mining counties north of Philadelphia that voted for Douglas. The Democrats don't seem to think Republicans will be fair with workingmen, so they're resisting incorporation into our government. When I got to Detroit, I read about a riot in Sandusky County, Ohio and a bigger on in the Democratic wards of Cincinnati. Kentucky men joined the fight for Cincy. Fremont sent in Ohio's Free State men with artillery to put them down. The fighting wrecked the part of town near the river, but it is said to be under our control now, what's left of it anyway. According to the Detroit paper, Fremont says that all of Ohio is now under Free State authority"

Lincoln looked up while feeding the horses. "Well, that's about the first good news I've heard from those parts. We won Ohio by less than a percent. If we can restore our authority there, we may be able to restore it over all of Illinois and Indiana. I couldn't stand to see the territorial integrity of any Free State disrupted, and the soil of any part opened to slavery."

"We'll do more than that, Father," Robert vowed. "We'll push our way down to New Orleans and open the Mississippi. One day we'll liberate the entire country. Fremont's just the man to do it, too. He's a Southern man by birth, but a Northern man by sentiment. Can you think of any man better to reunite this broken country in freedom?"

Lincoln laughed. "He's a fabulous flag designer too. I can't wait to see what sort of uniforms for our Free State Army he designs. That man has a flair for everything he does!"

Mrs. Lincoln came running through the open carriage house door holding a dripping umbrella. She gave Robert an enormous hug. "I thought I heard you two talking out here!" She pulled herself away from Robert. "Lord-a-mercy, if you aren't still growing! And you're soaked. Come on inside and get some hot coffee."

They entered their home through the back door into the kitchen, warm with the homey smells of coffee and roasting lamb. Tad and Willy ran screaming to hug Robert around the waist.

"I've got presents for both of you in my trunk!" Robert told them. "We'll bring it in after I have my coffee." The family sat down and began engaging in happy chatter about Robert's schooling in New Hampshire. Mary was at her conversational best, retelling stories of her girlhood schooling and then joking with Robert about being careful with all the ladies who were attracted to handsome educated young men.

Mr. Lincoln laughed as Mary and Robert outdid each other telling stories. As a student, Mr. Lincoln had never been near an institution of higher learning. His "education" came from the self-taught reading of Shakespeare, the Bible, the biography of George Washington, and the law. He was proud that his son would be on the way to Harvard after completing prep school.

The happy conversation took his mind away from his worries that the war might wreck so much of the Free States, including his own personal finances, that enrolling Robert at Harvard would not be possible. It banished his premonition that his family might soon be evacuating Springfield ahead of the return of Logan's Confederate Unionists who were being reinforced with militias from the South.

He had imagined fleeing with thousands of other Free State loyalists into northern Illinois carrying only the possessions they could load in their carriage, just like the pitiful evacuation of the Confederate Unionists who had followed Logan's men out of town during their retreat from Springfield. But Grant's fortifications south of town were strong, and the men recruited from the Wide Awakes who manned them were resolute. Why should he not trust Grant and his gathering forces to keep the Confederates from advancing northward, and eventually drive them out of Illinois?

He was also bothered by doubts about whether he had acted wisely in acquiescing to Fremont's demands to issue those resolutions anticipating Free States Independence during the Second Free State Convention. Perhaps those declarations had incited Yancey's slave raid into Indiana, touching off the conflagration ripping through the country. His instincts were almost always right. Why had he gone against them in acquiescing to Fremont and Garrison?

Mrs. Lincoln had comforted him when he mentioned those worries at breakfast.

"Don't torture yourself, Father. Those Southern hotheads have been determined to break up this country for years. They would have found a way to do it no matter what happened in Cleveland. You are a man of peace. Others have brought about this calamity, not you."

Now he felt at peace as the family had dinner, then resumed their conversation in the sitting room. He listened to Mary and Robert while watching Tad and Willy play with the puzzles and games Robert had brought for them. He fell asleep in the big chair, waking

149

up late in the evening after the rest of the family had retired to their rooms. He fell back into restful sleep, warmed by the fire.

The sun had been up an hour when there came a knock on the front door. Being still suspicious of danger after the recent partisan fighting, he asked the caller to identify himself. It was Congressman John Sherman. Sherman politely apologized for the early morning appearance, saying he should have arrived yesterday afternoon but was delayed by backed up traffic on the railroads. He got down to business as soon as Lincoln admitted him into the residence:

"I am here to inform you that, by order of the Free State Congress, Provisional President Fremont's term of office has expired. By the unanimous consent of the Free State Congress you are hereby notified that you have been elected President of the United States of Free America."

22

Cleveland, Ohio, July 4th, 1861

Cump Sherman and his brother John mingled with the inaugural guests on the lawn of one of the great mansions lining Cleveland's broad Euclid Avenue. The leafy scent from the dense northeastern Ohio forest encroaching on the edges of the city was in the air. A fresh breeze blew in off Lake Erie, coloring the sky with the deep hue characteristic of lake-cooled air. The city was as beautiful in summer as it was gloomy in winter. It was going to be a glorious inauguration day.

"Never thought I'd be attending two presidential inaugurations in one year," said John. "This one isn't as elegant as the Democrats', but I suppose it's not a bad start. Being as we're a new country we've had to learn to do everything from scratch."

"The next thing you'd better learn how to do," replied Cump, "is defend yourselves from the armies Douglas is assembling to reclaim you. For some reason he wants you renegades back in the Union."

"Renegades?" John laughed. "It doesn't sound like you're ready to come over to our camp just yet."

"Well, hell's bells, it didn't even seem like a real country from Louisiana," retorted Cump. "Now that I'm here the 'country' seems more substantial. By the way, what did Fremont do to get himself deposed? He was still your president when I left Louisiana."

"His arrogance did him in," answered John, almost laughing. "He surrounded himself with an entourage of pomposities. To get to Fremont you had to get past his Chief of Staff. To get to the Chief of Staff you had to interview the 'Adletus to the Chief of Staff.' He must have thought he was Provisional Grand Potentate. But, you know, I don't think he really wanted to be President. He wants a military command. It will be up to President Lincoln to decide whether he gets one."

"I was fairly well acquainted with Fremont in California," Cump reminisced. "He's one of those people who are loved or hated. I got along swimmingly with him, but I know plenty of others who didn't for precisely those reasons you mentioned. At any rate he's one of our bravest men. President Lincoln might well be justified in trusting him with a command."

John was astonished that Cump said '*our* bravest men.' Was he now beginning to consider himself a Free State citizen?

"You're right about his being brave," John agreed. "Even if he wasn't suited to being a permanent President, he did make a good start of things. Irwin McDowell has restored order in northern Ohio. Don Carlos Buell went with him to blast the Confederates out of Cincinnati. Grant got us back Central Illinois, and Lew Wallace recovered Indianapolis. These were all Fremont's appointments. When Fremont got back from Cincinnati he took the field and stabilized the front around New York City. And our new flag and national seals are his designs. Splendid work, indeed. But now it is time to get on to the business of civil government. Lincoln is the right man for that job."

That remains to be seen. Cump wanted to say it but held his tongue. He did not think highly of Lincoln, based on what he knew about him, which mostly came from the hostile Louisiana papers that painted Lincoln as a simple-minded hick.

Sherman noted that Fremont had taken appropriate measures to assure Mr. Lincoln's safety. Every intersection was patrolled by men wearing the blue Free State armbands with gold stars. They were searching anyone who looked suspicious. If one looked carefully, one could see the sharpshooters Fremont had posted on the roofs of all the mansions up and down Euclid Avenue. Cump hoped none were trigger happy enough to go shooting at innocent bystanders. But the men had to be there to protect against any remaining Douglas partisans bent on assassinating the first president of the United States of Free America.

Cump saw many rough looking men, no doubt Douglas voters, who might have been prone to making trouble if Fremont had not taken these precautions. He wondered whether the Free State Republic could maintain its existence long enough to win the loyalty of these men.

Mr. Lincoln will have to govern firmly enough to keep the Douglas men from rising up against him. But he must not come down on them so hard as to incite them into becoming subversive agents of the Confederates. If he walks the fine line between these extremes, their loyalty might become firmly attached to the new country.

Cump's attention returned to the inaugural party. He saw William Seward, who would be moving into the Cabinet as Lincoln's Secretary of State, pouting and rolling his eyes under a magnificent oak tree while being harangued by the dour Abolitionist Senators Charles Sumner and Ben Wade.

Mrs. Lincoln apparently noticed Seward's discomfort too, for she went to rescue him. She clasped Sumner's arm and began engaging the group in a cheery conversation about the entertainment arranged for tonight's Inaugural Ball. At once Sumner's appearance brightened. Even sour old Ben Wade began laughing. Leaving Sumner and Wade in good cheer, Mrs. Lincoln graciously escorted Seward over to meet her nieces whom she had invited to Cleveland to assist her in her duties as First Lady. Seward was smiling too as he tipped his hat in greeting Mrs. Lincoln's lovely nieces.

Cump looked back at John then turned toward Mrs. Lincoln's party. "Mrs. Lincoln is lacking nothing in the social graces," he commented. "That's a handy trait for Mr. Lincoln's government."

John had noticed it too. "Yes, indeed, Mrs. Lincoln has been a ray of sunshine in an otherwise gloomy season. She's one of those people who can't help but inspire optimism and good cheer. Maybe she'll be able to woo the foreign dignitaries too. That will be important in getting us recognized as a nation."

At 11:45 Mr. Lincoln, the members of the Free State Congress, and the newly reconstituted Supreme Court walked in line to the inaugural platform set up in the middle of Euclid Avenue. All waited while Mr. Lincoln gave his inaugural speech. The new Supreme Court Chief Justice David Davis stood ready to administer the Oath of Office. Davis was a far cry from the Confederate Union's slave-mongering Chief Justice Roger Taney of *Dred Scott Decision* notoriety, whom Lincoln would have been sure to have tangled with had he been elected President of the old United States.

Lincoln began speaking. Cump noted that his voice was not deep but was nevertheless strong enough to make itself heard for blocks down Euclid Avenue.

Fellow-Citizens of the United States of Free America:

I appear before you to address you briefly and to take in your presence the oath prescribed by the Constitution. This occasion is both continuity and a new beginning.

It is continuity because our United Free States are organized under the same Constitution as were all our previous national governments going back to the inauguration of our first President seventy-two years ago. We have changed not a single word of that Constitution, adding only the 13th and 14th Amendments that shall forever abolish slavery within our present territory and all future territories that our Free State Republic may acquire, and shall provide for equal protection under the law for all citizens of the United States of Free America.

It is a new beginning because any people anywhere, being so inclined and having the power, have the right to rise up and shake off the existing government, and form a new one that suits them better. This is a most sacred right, a right which we hope and believe, is to liberate the world.

*We **have** been so inclined to rise up and dissociate ourselves from that government which now styles itself "The Confederate Union." We have done so because that government has rejected, by the repeated actions of its Chief Executive, its Congress, and its Courts, our founding principle that "All men are created equal and are endowed by their Creator with certain inalienable rights."*

That government has rejected this founding principle in favor of the new one it claims to have discovered in the Dred Scott Decision --- the decision declaring, in Chief Justice Taney's words, Negroes to be "so far inferior that they have no rights which the white man is bound to respect; that the Negro might justly and lawfully be reduced to slavery and treated as an ordinary article of merchandise and traffic whenever a profit can be made by it."

That government has asserted this principle as the basis of its pretended right to enter the Free States to kidnap and enslave as many free persons of color as any of its white citizens may desire. This desire was put into effect when an armed party invaded our free soil, kidnapped free Negroes without obtaining the necessary court orders for their removal, and then fired upon and killed the Free State men who interdicted them. When the orchestrators of this scheme were interdicted the

154

government of the "Confederate Union" called upon its Army to become an accomplice not only in the kidnapping of free Negroes, but in the deaths of the Free State men who sought to prevent their kidnapping.

It is impossible for us to remain associated with any government that orders its Army to kill free men who dare to protect their fellow free citizens from being sold into slavery.

This so-called "Confederate Union" desires not only to subjugate the Free States that were formerly in union with it, but to conquer the neighboring free Republics of Mexico and Central America to impose slavery upon **them**. It has provoked not only the hostility of the free peoples in this hemisphere, but also of the most formidable Powers of Europe who have vowed to oppose, by all necessary measures including war, the enslavement of the people of any free country.

It is impossible for us to remain associated with a government that would involve us in its wars to impose slavery upon free peoples.

Let us now compare the condition of our present generation to the generation of our Founders. In 1776 our Founders severed their ties to the British Crown, citing many specific grievances. Today we find these same grievances they rebelled against imposed upon us by the Confederate Union. In addition must be added the kidnapping of free citizens and enslaving them, an outrage that even King George did not dare to inflict on his American Colonists.

Today, when four generations have passed since that Revolution, we find that the British have abolished slavery in all their Dominions. The so-called Confederate Union alone, of all the English-speaking peoples, continues not only to defend slavery but seeks to expand it, by all measures including war. Before our dissociation from the Confederate Union our free citizens of color could only assure their freedom by removing themselves from our country and emigrating northeast to the lands beyond our borders where the people are governed by the Queen of that very Empire our Founders rebelled against!

And now consider Mexico. In 1835 American settlers in Texas rebelled because they felt that their rights under the Mexican Constitution had been violated by the Dictator Santa Anna. Yet even Santa Anna did not seek to kidnap any free man in Texas and sell him into slavery. Today we find not a single slave in Mexico. Yet the leaders of the government known as the Confederate Union have fixed themselves upon the conquest of Mexico. They claim to be acting from the humanitarian motive of wanting to "restore order" to that troubled country. Their design is to conquer the land, dispossessing its free inhabitants, and resettling the country with slaves and slave masters! That is **their** definition of "humanitarian," but it must never be **ours!**

The crowd, which until this point had followed the custom of respectful silence, began to cheer.

"What do you think of Mr. Lincoln now?" John whispered to his brother.

"I'll let you know when he's finished," answered Cump.

155

Responding to the cheering crowd, Lincoln began speaking extemporaneously, which he did not often do, especially on such a momentous occasion. He put down his prepared speech and began talking directly to the people.

I am wondering, now, what those illustrious men of 1776 who pledged their lives, their fortunes, and their sacred honor to vindicate their Declaration that all men are created equal would think of the government that calls itself "The Confederate Union." I am wondering whether George Washington and his men suffering cold and hunger in Valley Forge would be proud of that government. I wonder whether Thomas Jefferson, author of not only that Declaration, but also of the great Ordinance of 1787 that forbade the spread of slavery north of the Ohio River, would be proud of that government. Would Patrick Henry, Thomas Paine, Sam Adams, John Adams, and James Madison be proud of that government?

"They would not!" roared crowd.

If they lived today would they stand with the Confederate Union? Or would they stand with us?

"With us!" the crowd roared louder.

And did these Founders dream of founding a great Republic that would shine its light of liberty as a beacon to liberate the oppressed peoples of the earth, or did they dream of founding a Slave Empire dedicated to oppressing the free peoples of the earth? What did they dream of --- the liberation of Mankind or its enslavement?"

"Liberation!"

And there is one other thing that I must ask you to consider: The President of the so-called Confederate Union says the principle of his government is that men of lighter color may make slaves of men of darker color. He starts by saying that Whites may make slaves of Negroes. Then he expands the concept to include Mexicans, Indians, Chinese, Japanese, and mulattos among his "inferior races." He says that the men who presume themselves to belong to the most intelligent race have a "sacred right of self government" to enslave the men of those races that they presume to be less intelligent.

With all this quibbling about which man is entitled to make a slave of another --- by color, intelligence, or some other accidental characteristic of birth --- is there any person in this country who is safe from enslavement? Is every other man to become the slave of the one who has the lightest skin? Is every other man to become the slave of the one presumed to be more intelligent? And how can we be sure that the day will not come when the person of modest wealth must become the slave of the person who has more?

*Is this not **opposite** to the principle that founded the United States of America, that "All men are created equal and are endowed by their Creator with certain inalienable rights, that among these are life....liberty....and the pursuit of happiness!" Is this the principle for all men, or only some?*

"For all!"

*And is it a principle of the Confederate Union or of the United States of **Free** America!*

"The United States of **Free** America!"

Many people were shouting with Lincoln, including the rough-looking men Cump had presumed to be Douglas voters.

Did the millions who came here fleeing oppression intend for themselves to become masters of a Slave Empire?

"They did not!"

*Do **you** want to be part of a slave empire?*

"We do not!"

*Will you pledge your lives, your fortunes, and your sacred honor to save this **Free Republic**, to pass it down to future generations of free American citizens, just as the Founders pledged **their** lives, **their** fortunes, and **their** sacred honor to pass it down to us?*

"We pledge it!"

*"The United States of **Free** America!"*

"The United States of **Free** America!"

"Well, you win," said Cump to his brother, as the crescendo of noise faded. "I have made up my mind to take an Oath of Loyalty as a citizen of the United States of **Free** America!"

23

The White House, Washington City
July 15, 1861

Vice President Jefferson Davis paced the Executive Office on the second floor of the White House while waiting for the arrival of Robert E. Lee. He was standing in for President Douglas, who'd taken ill yesterday, an infirmity likely aggravated by the stress of seeing his country unravel.

This place is ever so dreary without Douglas. Hope the old boy gets well enough to be back here tomorrow. Thank goodness General Lee will soon be here to breathe some life into it until Douglas gets back.

Lee had been out West for the last five weeks, stabilizing the chaotic military frontier out there. The Free State's professional military men, notably Nathaniel Lyon, U.S. Grant, and John Schofield, had tried to push the Confederate Union out of Indiana and Illinois, and drive them south of the Missouri River west of St. Louis. Lee had bucked up the commands of the Confederate Union's spirited but amateur commanders Sterling Price and John "Blackjack" Logan. He had then gone on to Indiana to help General Harney patch together a line held by Indiana and Kentucky militiamen and the Regular Army men who had fallen back from Delphi.

With the West stabilized, Davis and McClellan called Lee back East to lead the main offensive against the Free States around New York and Philadelphia. It would begin at noon tomorrow unless the Free States responded to Douglas' ultimatum to return to the Confederate Union. There would be a general amnesty for those who pledged to refrain from further insurrection. Those who had lost property in the partisan fighting would be made whole. Davis didn't expect the Free States to accept the ultimatum, nor did he particularly want them to.

*We must suppress the Abolitionists once and for all and reconstruct the Free States on **our** terms. They must understand that we are a Confederate Union of Slave States and Free States, not the unitary government of Free States that the Abolitionists and Republicans desire, and which they would have tried to consummate if Mr. Lincoln had been elected. The Abolitionists are crazy to think we would ever force slavery upon their Free States. But they must be taught to honor their Constitutional duty to help us catch our runaway slaves.*

Davis saw himself, McClellan, and Lee as the greatest troika of military commanders in history. He and McClellan were developing the plans for campaigning in the East. Knowing McClellan's fondness for obscuring the larger picture with tedious details, he wanted to brief Lee before bringing him over to the War Department.

At midmorning, Douglas' secretary announced Lee's arrival. Davis sprang from his chair, embracing Lee as one of the few men he would have honored with more than a formal handshake. "Welcome home, General Lee! I trust you are enjoying a pleasant visit with your family at Arlington. Please give my best regards to Mrs. Lee."

"Thank you, Mr. Vice President. Yes, I had a most pleasant homecoming on Sunday. Mrs. Lee and the family are fine. The house and the land are in good condition. Please excuse my tardiness this morning, but I could not avoid tending to some last minute home business."

"It is quite all right. I'm only sorry that the time you had with your family was so brief. We'll be asking you to take the field again tomorrow, if the Free States have given no satisfactory response to the President's offer."

"To take the offensive?" asked Lee.

159

"Yes," answered Davis. "We'll be discussing it with McClellan. I regret President Douglas won't be with us, but his health will not allow it. His doctor positively forbids him seeing visitors today."

Lee did not disguise his alarm. "I didn't realize his health was so unsettled. The country especially needs him at this moment. Is there any estimate as to when he might be well enough to join us?"

Davis sighed in exasperation. "The Good Lord only knows. He has been laid low by typhoid, like many others in this city. If he survives the next week he should be out of the woods." The alternative "if he **doesn't** survive" went unspoken. "We should never have built our capital in this fetid swamp. When this war is over we must ask Congress to remove the capital to a healthier place, perhaps to a new Federal District in the Catoctin Mountains."

"Yes, we certainly should do that," Lee replied, thinking of the military implications. "This place is not only unhealthy but all too vulnerable to seaborne attack. A new capital in the mountains would be infinitely more defensible, plus a necessary improvement in health, and an inspiration at all seasons. It would be a fitting monument to our reunited Confederate Union."

"We'll have to move the White House and the Capitol brick by brick," Davis mused. "But we should get started on it as soon as the war is over. Let's not wait until the fevers in this place incapacitate our entire government." His thoughts returned to Douglas, whose health had been dealt two blows in Washington City: first by the rampant fevers festering the swampy ground, and then by the tribulations of national crisis that would have drained the strength of even a healthy man.

Douglas should have taken my advice to go up to a spa in the Catoctin Mountains for a couple days' rest. He needs to be relaxing in the hot springs instead of staying here over-drinking and allowing constant worries to interrupt his sleep. There is only so much a body can stand.

The possibility that Douglas might not recover unnerved him. He tried not to show his concern to General Lee.

The men seated themselves. "Douglas has ordered a campaign to recover the Free States," Davis informed him. "It will begin tomorrow noon if his deadline for the Free

States to return voluntarily passes unheeded. McClellan will give you a full briefing, but fundamentally, he's worked out a plan of general mobilization that he believes will allow for us to reestablish our authority over the Free States in a 90-day campaign."

"I wanted to ask the President about that," Lee interjected. "I wanted to ask him if he is certain it will be advantageous to us to reclaim the Free States by force. I believe we could restore peace immediately by offering them their independence based on a mutually agreeable boundary. Should we not let them go their own way, just as our Southern States would want to leave if we had discovered our position in the Union to be untenable? Do we desire anyone in the Confederate Union who doesn't want to be here?"

Davis suppressed a grimace. *If Douglas gets his way, we're going to force a lot of people into the Confederate Union --- everybody south of the Rio Grande and north of the Great Lakes. But to get to the Mexicans and Canadians we'll have to put down our own Free State Rebels first.*

"That was my original thought too," Davis counselled. "Let the Yankees go off into their own country if that's what they want. Douglas has persuaded me that would not bring peace."

Lee raised his eyebrows. "Then he is a persuasive man indeed! I have heard you argue most convincingly, over many years, that the states are the people's sovereign governments."

Davis smiled as if to acknowledge that his past speeches advocating state sovereignty and the right of secession now sounded strange even to his own ears.

"I have come to agree with Douglas that this is a partisan civil war instigated by the 37% who voted for the Republicans against the 63% who voted for us. On principle it doesn't matter whether the 37% are concentrated in one group of states or are evenly distributed. No matter where the minority is situated, the majority is sovereign over every inch of the country."

"That contradicts the principle of state sovereignty," said Lee. "But I am aware that Presidents Jackson, Jefferson, Madison, and Washington came to accept it. My father also accepted it when he undertook Washington's commission to put down the Whiskey

Rebellion. His States Rights friends in Virginia never forgave him. His decision cost him everything, ultimately even his life."

Davis answered thoughtfully. "Your father was a wise and courageous man. I can well imagine the torment he felt in placing his loyalty to the nation ahead of his States Rights friends. But he knew the national government would have fallen if it had not asserted its authority. Sustaining the national government was the correct decision then as now."

Lee was stunned into silence on hearing Davis take the position entirely opposite to what he'd said in all the years before. Davis went on to reinforce his point, his explanation aimed at convincing himself as much as Lee.

"Douglas believes the country belongs not only to us in the present time, but to all the generations yet to come. He thinks we will have a fair run at the ballot box in all the northern states. He says industrial workers in the North are not Abolitionists. They are men of modest means who fear that if slaves are freed, the Negroes will come north and take their jobs. Douglas says we will become their party, as we are the party of Southern yeoman farmers. We must reclaim the country for their sakes as well as ours."

Lee was impressed by the Unionist influence Douglas had made on Davis. "It appears you have found these arguments irrefutable."

"Douglas makes one other vital point," Davis expounded. He waved his hand expansively over the wall map. "He says this is *our* continent. Until we divided among ourselves the European Empires respected Monroe's Doctrine. They did not dare to intervene anywhere on the American Continents, let alone on our own borders. Now the British are reinforcing the Canadas. The French are on their way into Mexico. How can we be secure with the French Imperialists controlling Mexico, the British fielding an army in Canada, and the Free States left alone to seek an alliance with them? The Mexicans, Canadians, British, and French are every bit as hostile to slavery as Yankee Abolitionists. If we don't reclaim the Free States, and fast, we are going to have a five-sided antislavery alliance opposing us."

"I had not thought of that," Lee acknowledged. "A five-sided alliance with the Free States *would* pose a material threat to us. President Douglas has thought through this issue more thoroughly than me. I suppose that is why we elected him President."

"Douglas believes we must reclaim the Free States before they subvert our voters," Davis added emphatically. "They appear to be making progress in that direction in Ohio, where we have reports of our voters enlisting in their so-called Free State Army. If they acquire the loyalty of our voters, their manpower may become too much for us to contend with. Indeed, they might threaten *us* with invasion, especially if they receive help from Britain and France."

"Thank you for your explanation, Mr. Vice President," answered Lee. "I am clear now on why we must recover the whole of the Free States."

Davis motioned toward the door. "Well, then, what say we go to the War Department and have a palaver with Mac."

24

The War Department, Washington City
July 15, 1861

McClellan studied the map spread over his desk while he waited for Lee and Davis. It was a railway map of the East from the Atlantic Coast to the first tier of states beyond the Mississippi. He preferred these railroad company maps to the typologically-detailed ones produced by the Army's engineers. His experience as an observer of the Crimean War had educated him to understand that railroads were essential to supply modern armies, whose expenditures of ammunition and rations were prodigious.

This will be an economic as well as military war. Railroads are the arteries of both. The side that can organize its railroads most effectively to bring the largest number of men and equipment to the critical points of battle, will prevail.

He had labeled his railroad map ***"General Plan for Suppressing the Free State Insurrection."*** He had divided it with a grease pencil into new military departments designed to facilitate the prosecution of war against the insurgent Free States. He had then demarcated the military frontier between the territories held by the Confederate Union and the United States of Free America with a blue pencil:

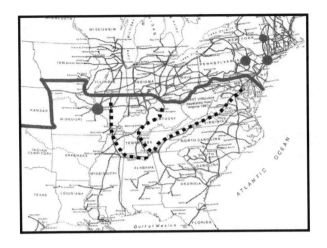

The contiguous military frontier followed the rounded tip of Delaware across the northern border of Maryland. The line bulged up west of Philadelphia where Confederate partisans in Maryland had crossed the state line to help their Democratic-voting friends in southern Pennsylvania. There, the military frontier split York and Adams counties where Confederate Unionist partisans battled Free Staters for control of the county seats of York and Gettysburg. West of Gettysburg the frontier followed the Pennsylvania line. It then followed the Virginia panhandle as far as Wheeling, falling short of the far-northern portion of the panhandle occupied by Free State men keeping the railroad from Pittsburgh to Ohio open. It then followed the Ohio River to the Indiana line.

Ohio particularly concerned McClellan, not least because he still had a residence in Cincinnati from his days as president of the Ohio and Mississippi Railroad. Ohio had voted for Lincoln by the slim margin of 50.8%. However, Ohio did not have its Democratic vote concentrated in the southern counties as did Indiana and Illinois. Most of the Ohio River counties, except several near Cincinnati, were Republican-heavy and therefore blocked the Douglas men in Kentucky from coming across the river to help their Ohio friends. The Douglas votes were concentrated in only two small parts of the state, neither having a charismatic leader like John Logan in Illinois or Fernando Wood in New York City.

The uprisings by Democratic voters against Republican authority in Ohio had therefore taken on the character of mob riots instead of organized efforts. Governor Dennison and Provisional President Fremont had suppressed the riot of Douglas men in, of

165

all unlikely places, Fremont, Ohio --- so named a decade before to honor Fremont for his explorations of the West!

Dennison and Fremont had next embarked on the heavy-handed suppression of the Douglas men in the riverfront wards of Cincinnati. About a third of the city had been demolished, depending on whose story you believed, either by Fremont's promiscuous artillery bombardment or by fires set by intoxicated Douglas rioters, probably by both. McClellan had no word whether his residence in the city had survived, and if it had, whether the Free State Government had confiscated it.

The aspect of the map of most concern to McClellan was the Free State Rebels' blockage of the Baltimore and Ohio Railroad running from Washington to Cincinnati and then to St. Louis. Without possession of that railroad, the Confederate Union was divided in two by the Appalachian Mountains, over which no railroads crossed. The only routes from Washington and Baltimore to Louisville and St. Louis connected through Chattanooga and Stevenson, Alabama, a thousand-mile detour. McClellan and drawn dotted lines over the long detour routes into Louisville and St. Louis.

West of Cincinnati the military frontier traced the Ohio River, being anchored by the Abolitionist-settled town of Madison, Indiana. West of Madison it bulged northward into Indiana along the Confederate-held Louisville, New Albany, and Chicago railroad. It then jogged northwest, stopping just short of Indianapolis, held by Free State militias reinforced from Michigan and Ohio. From there it ran west to Terre Haute, then doglegged north up the Wabash until it encountered Grant's fortified line along the Toledo, Wabash and Great Western railroad. It continued along that line through Central Illinois from Danville to Springfield to Quincy. The Free Staters had won the partisan street brawl for Springfield but were defeated in the pitched battle between John Logan's Democrat militias and U.S. Grant's Free Staters at Carlinville to the Southwest. The military frontier had stabilized in between.

It then followed the Mississippi River up past the top of Missouri, continuing from there along the Missouri/Iowa border until it reached the Nebraska Territory where the map ended. West of Missouri sprawled the Kansas Territory, the scene of brutal guerilla fighting between pro-slavery and Free-Soil men during the "Bleeding Kansas" violence of the 1850s. Free-Soil men had gotten the better of it, destining Kansas to become a free state, while the pro-slavery men either moved on or acquiesced. McClellan did not want that violence to get started up again. There were only a hundred thousand settlers out there, not enough to threaten the Confederate Union. He decided to leave them alone for the time being while he worked toward defeating the Eastern centers of the Free State Rebellion.

West of Kansas there were no disturbances, other than the usual Indian raids. The Pacific Coast, with its 70% Democrat majorities and Southern-rights governors, was quiet for the moment. There were rumors of unrest by Yankee emigrants in San Francisco, but their leaders were arrested before being able to organize any serious trouble. No doubt Fremont would have been one of the ringleaders if he had not come east to lead the Free State Rebellion from Ohio.

McClellan had drawn in three blue circles in the Northeast to show centers of Confederate Union authority remaining north of the contiguous frontier.

The first was Metropolitan New York City, encompassing the city, neighboring Brooklyn, Long Island, the suburbs in New Jersey, and those going up the Hudson. This was a strongly Democratic and therefore pro-Confederate area whose constituents were largely immigrant workingmen who had little use for Negroes or their Republican benefactors, and merchants who made most of their money trading with Southern planters. Mayor Fernando Wood, a staunch Confederate Unionist, had ordered his supporters to suppress the Republican Wide Awakes before they could organize against his administration. About two hundred thousand Free Staters had left the city and its environs, the rest subsiding into quiet neutrality. Horace Greeley, like many others nominally loyal to the Free States, stayed on in New York, continuing to publish his paper without endorsing either side.

The evacuation of the city's Free State loyalists was mitigated by the arrival of about the same number of Douglas voters from the areas of New York and New England controlled by Free Staters. This exchange of population all along the military frontier was hardening the divide between Confederate Unionists and the Free Staters. Many refugees, fleeing burned out homes and mourning friends and relatives killed in partisan fighting, had vengeance on their minds. It was becoming ever more difficult for anyone to remain neutral.

From McClellan's perspective, the most significant effect of the blue circle around Metropolitan New York was the occupation of the Free States' primary seaport and its interconnecting railroad terminals. This disrupted the Free States' communications as much as their occupation of the Baltimore and Ohio disrupted the Confederate Union's.

The Free States were left with only two circuitous, overloaded railroad routes linking the Republican strongholds in New England to those around the Great Lakes. Their overseas trade was reduced to products produced in New England having access to local ports. The vast harvests of the Great Lakes States could not reach any port for exportation to Europe, thereby diminishing what little was left of the Free States' foreign exchange. Equally important was the loss of financial capital the Confederate Union's grip on New York denied to the Free States. Although some banks and trading companies owned by Republicans had relocated their operations to Boston or Cleveland, most decided to stay put and take their chances in the Confederate Union.

He had shaded in another disconnected blue circle around the coal mining counties of eastern Pennsylvania where Confederate Union partisans controlled the countryside around Reading and Easton, further constricting Philadelphia's railroad communications to the north and west. In the national election, Philadelphia had voted a slight Confederate Unionist majority. But two years prior it had elected staunch Republican Mayor Alexander Henry dedicated to keeping Philadelphia in the Free States.

McClellan's blue area in eastern Pennsylvania was separated from the blue circle around Metropolitan New York by a corridor Free State Republicans had managed to drive through western New Jersey and eastern Pennsylvania. The corridor was just wide enough to maintain communications between Philadelphia and the Free State "mainland" via the Delaware River and the railroad and highway beside it.

Within the territory held by the Confederate Union, McClellan had placed a red circle over St. Louis, where U.S. Army Captain Nathaniel Lyon's Free State men and their German auxiliaries were still fighting. McClellan did not expect them to last much longer now that Grant's attempt to relieve them had failed. Until they surrendered, they would continue to tie down Missouri Governor Claiborne Jackson's Confederate Union militias, thereby preventing their transfer to the main front in Central Illinois.

McClellan began placing silver three-cent coins on the map to show his points of military concentration. He fancied this coin because its front side was embossed with a large star enclosing the Shield of the Union at its center.

He placed the first coins over Metropolitan New York City where most omen in the Regular Army garrisons stationed at the harbor forts and the Brooklyn Navy Yard remained loyal to the Confederate Union. These garrisons, augmented by Mayor Fernando Wood's New York City Militia, manned the fortified checkpoints on the perimeter around the city. General Joseph Johnston had recently arrived to command the Military District of New York and Northern New Jersey.

He placed another coin over the U.S. Military Academy at West Point, a couple dozen miles beyond the fortified lines around Metro New York. It was held by a Confederate Union garrison commanded by Superintendent P.G.T. Beauregard. The fighting around the academy had inspired Beauregard to design the Confederate Union's battle flag to distinguish his men from the Free Staters who for a time had continued to fly the old United States flag.

He placed his next coins around Baltimore and Wilmington where militia companies forwarded by the Governors of Delaware, Maryland, and Virginia were collecting. He had assigned that command to General Albert Sydney Johnston, recently arrived from his post in California. Further west, he placed a coin on Wheeling, Virginia to show the garrison of Regular Army men transferred from Pennsylvania's Carlisle Barracks.

In Indiana he placed a coin over Franklin, the station on the Louisville, New Albany, and Chicago Railroad just south of Indianapolis where General Harney's command had fallen back. There General Harney was accumulating Governor Hendricks' Indiana Militia, which had largely remained loyal to the Confederate Union, and the militia companies being forwarded by Kentucky's Governor Magoffin. Pending the outcome of the anticipated battle for Indianapolis, Governor Hendricks had removed his Confederate Union government to New Albany, while the Free States had installed their government headed by Oliver P. Morton in South Bend.

In Central Illinois he placed coins to show the partisans and militiamen accumulating under "Blackjack" Logan's command around the rail junctions between Vandalia and Charleston. He placed other coins around the red dot of St. Louis to show the

169

location of the 15,000 Missouri militiamen under Sterling Price's command trying to wrest control of the city from Nathaniel Lyon's Free State diehards.

McClellan considered the strategic plan he would be explaining to General Lee. Lee had already implemented the first part by stabilizing the front through Indiana, Illinois, and Missouri with training camps, supply lines, and fortifications. Now McClellan would begin the second part in the East by capturing Philadelphia, then linking up with the metropolitan New York exclave, then plunging into the Abolitionist heartland of New England.

With Douglas and Davis here to help me in Washington, and with General Lee commanding in the field, we will be able to move rapidly. We will befuddle the enemy and defeat him before he even knows what hit him. We will win this war, as we won the Mexican War, with maneuvers so rapid the enemy will not have time to choose his ground to make a stand. It will be a quick war with few men killed in battle or dying from the diseases that plague armies in static quarters.

He mused about how differently things might have been if Mr. Lincoln had been elected as the President who would call upon him to quell a Slave State Rebellion.

Mr. Lincoln is the 'original gorilla,' the fool of Republican Abolitionists. Were I to give him decisive victories he would make himself a Caesar. He would free the slaves by executive decree and then impose military rule over the South. I should have had to move exceedingly slowly in order to keep the howling, cackling mob of Abolitionists at bay. I should have had to give the Slave States time to decide to come back into the Union on their own volition....

He was roused from his reverie by a knocking on the door. It was Adjutant General Sam Cooper announcing the arrival of Lee and Davis.

25

The War Department, Washington City
July 15, 1861

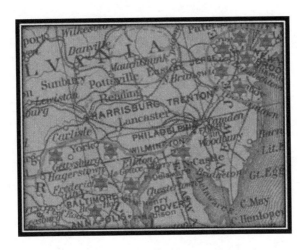

"Here come the warhorses!" exclaimed McClellan. He greeted Lee warmly, thanking him profusely for his success in the West and for keeping the War Department fully apprised of the situation out there. That Lee could win the confidence of such an egocentric man spoke to Lee's unimpeachable character of honor, courage, and judgment.

McClellan ushered Lee and Davis over to the map spread over his desk. Davis, seeing the three-cent pieces McClellan had stacked all over it, was amused.

"You didn't run out of coins, did you Mac? I'm sure General Lee wouldn't mind lending you the buttons on his uniform."

"Not these buttons!" exclaimed Lee in mock outrage. "How about if I ask my carpenter to whittle Mac some pieces he can use to mark our formations in detail, including corps and divisions? Recovering the Free States will be a big operation, and we might as well get started now in planning it properly."

"Thank you so very much, General Lee," replied McClellan. "Please ask your carpenter to whittle some arrows too, to indicate lines of advance. Ask him to paint the pieces in two colors --- blue to indicate our units, and red to indicate the insurgents'. Showing unit locations with carved pieces is so much clearer than drawing them in on the map."

Lee and Davis took a minute to peruse McClellan's map.

"Mac has done most of the planning for this operation," said Davis. "He'll explain what we've been thinking while you were busy in the West."

"Thank you," McClellan graciously replied, "but there's no need for you to be modest about your contributions. It was a collaborative effort. That's why it is a sound plan."

Lee smiled to himself. Here were two of the most egotistical personalities outdoing each other with praise.

This bodes well for the coming campaign. There will be no political infighting like we had in the Mexican War between President Polk and Generals Zachary Taylor and Winfield Scott. How can one expect the soldiers to give their lives in battle when their generals are intriguing against each other and the President? Lord knows, we have our share of difficult officers like Joe Johnston and Braxton Bragg, but I do not think they will be allowed to conspire against each other --- not when there is the cooperative leadership at the top by myself, Jefferson Davis, Secretary of War McClellan, and President Douglas.

On Davis' cue McClellan began explaining his strategic plans with his unique mixture of enthusiasm and pedagogic authority.

"General Lee, we plan to mobilize rapidly, advance into the Free States from directions they do not expect, and occupy their state capitals and important cities before they have time to organize against us."

He pointed along the line of coins he had stacked along the mid latitude of the country from New York City to Central Illinois.

"We've already redeployed the state militia companies called up for service in Mexico. If the Free States don't reply to the President's offer of reunion by tomorrow noon, a general mobilization of **national** volunteers will begin. Tomorrow will be designated as M-day, the day of mobilization. By M+90 our plan is to have the National Authority restored to all insurgent areas from Maine to Minnesota."

172

Lee's face showed a trace of skepticism. "That's an ambitious schedule, Mac. Besides engaging the Free State Insurgents we'll need to garrison the recovered areas and organize them under military government until civil authority can be restored. We must expect to detach men to guard our lines of communication. And remember, we'll have about a quarter of our men on sick call until they are inured to camp diseases. Given those considerations, are you certain ninety days will be sufficient to conclude the campaign?"

"Yes," replied McClellan with confidence. He had expected this question. "We have the manpower required for the task. Please bear with me while I explain the numbers, because they are the foundation of the plan."

McClellan picked up the notes on his desk and glanced at them as he explained the plan of mobilization.

"The Confederate Union has within our military frontiers almost the entire population of the Slave States, which are 8,300,000 Whites plus 3,500,000 slaves. In addition, we have 1,500,000 within our lines in Metropolitan New York. We have around 400,000 loyal Pennsylvanians. We have about 400,000 loyal persons in the counties we occupy in Indiana and about 500,000 in Illinois. We have another 600,000 in California and Oregon but it is not practical to bring any large number east in time to get them into the war. Those who want to volunteer are welcome to do so, but they must pay their own fare to come east."

McClellan paused to see if Lee wanted to question these numbers. Lee nodded his acceptance.

"That means we have just over eleven million Whites within our military frontier," McClellan elaborated. "Assuming that about 10% are able-bodied men of military age, we may expect to have 300,000 men in the field by M+30 and 500,000 by M+60. We already have on hand at the points I designated about 100,000 men who will be ready to commence operations tomorrow noon if no word of capitulation from the Free States is received by then."

Lee again nodded his understanding.

"Now let us count the resources of our adversaries. The Free States excluding California and Oregon have a population of 18,500,000. Inside their military frontier they have about 16,000,000. Lincoln won about 55% of their vote. That means they have a little less than 9,000,000 whose loyalty they can count on. We must occupy their territory before they have time to mobilize their loyal population for military service. Nor can we allow them time to win the loyalty of the population who voted for us. That's why a ninety-day campaign is essential."

McClellan pointed to the map. "Our first objective will be the recovery of Philadelphia."

Lee noted McClellan's use of the word "recovery" instead of "capture." President Douglas had gotten across the idea that the Free States were a part of the Confederate Union, not an alien country.

McClellan pointed to the coins covering Metro New York.

"We're feigning an attack from here to make the Free Staters concentrate their men into lines facing New York. They'll try to fight us close to New York because an advance from there will sever Philly's communications with New England, making the city untenable."

McClellan tapped his finger on the coins around Baltimore.

"We're feigning another attack from Baltimore through Wilmington and into Philadelphia from the southwest. They are fortifying the line of Darby and Cobbs Creek south of town to oppose it. We've thrown them off the scent of our real axis of advance"

He displayed a boyishly devious grin and waved his finger at Lee.

"Davis and I have in mind, pending your concurrence, that the main advance into Philly will be from the west, by way of Harrisburg. When we occupy Harrisburg, we'll have the State Capital and control of the Penn Central. The Penn Central will open Philly's back door. If we can occupy the city before the Free Staters know what hit them, we'll prevent a costly street-for-street battle like the one in St. Louis that would wear down our army and wreck the city. We'll capture the Free State militias on the Darby Creek Line from the rear, then wheel north to capture those on the New York City front. What do you think?"

Lee studied the map. "This appears to be a carefully considered and very daring, yet practical, plan. How long do you estimate it will take to reach Harrisburg, and from there how long into Philadelphia?"

McClellan was ebullient. General Lee's approval enthused him more than his extraordinary self confidence already had.

"The movement has already commenced. Davis and I took the liberty of ordering an advance guard to occupy the county seat towns of York and Gettysburg, which was accomplished yesterday afternoon. I hope you will take no offense at our precipitate action, but it wasn't possible to relay the order through you while you were in transit."

"That's quite all right," responded Lee. "You acted as duty required with Douglas incapacitated and me out of contact. I doubt that any of us will be able to stay current with events along the entire front from Iowa to New York. We must show initiative to act as circumstances demand."

"Thank you, General Lee," replied Davis. "I don't need to tell you that most of our generals would throw a hissy fit if the Vice President and Secretary of War by-passed their chain of command."

"We can't afford 'hissy fits' when the nation is in danger," said Lee gravely. "We don't have even a moment to waste in second-guessing each other. We are all working to restore peace and harmony to our divided country. That must be our exclusive object."

McClellan and Davis looked at each other. Each understood this characteristic of Lee's greatness, in giving his total consideration to the success of the operation and none to any perceived offenses against his personal prerogatives as General of the Army.

McClellan resumed his explanation of the plan by pointing at the map.

"It's thirty miles from Gettysburg to Harrisburg. We aim to be in Harrisburg on M+2. We'll secure the Susquehanna crossing at Wrightsville on M+3, giving us the short route into Philly, which we expect to reach on M+4. With any luck, the Free Staters won't know we're coming to Philly until our men are detraining in the terminal."

"You're certain we have enough men available to hold on to these places after we occupy them?" Lee asked.

"We have nearly forty thousand armed men in camps around Baltimore with more arriving every day," McClellan answered with authority. "There are enough Regular Army men to stiffen them.

"I've got twenty-five hundred men in Gettysburg and another twenty-five hundred in York. I put another five thousand on the trains running up there today. I'll be moving the same number tomorrow. The rest will be put on the march to Wrightsville. We'll have ten thousand men to garrison Harrisburg and thirty thousand more to pour into Philly's back door.

"While we're entering Philly from the west, Albert Johnston will be threatening from Wilmington and Joe Johnston from New York. The Free Staters won't know which way to turn. They may surrender once we're in the city. When they do, move your men past the city and up into New Jersey. Attack the Free State men besieging New York from the rear while Joe Johnston pins their front. If the Free State Insurrection does not surrender, +we will commence further operations to close it out. In that event, you might return to the West and assume direct command of the combined forces of Sterling Price, Blackjack Logan, and William Harney."

"Of course, those decisions will be yours as General-in-Chief," confirmed Jefferson Davis. "Your presence at any point on our line will be sure to inspire confidence, efficiency, and the most complete victory."

"Your leadership will also be necessary to maintain discipline," McClellan added. "We've had some ugly incidents in this partisan fighting. I want that clamped down on. We must scrupulously obey the traditions of civilized warfare as we did during the Mexican War. After the Mexicans found out we were fair with them, they sold supplies to our army and helped us to suppress the irregulars. That's how we must treat our misguided fellow citizens in the Free States. Let them know they'll be treated as citizens of a common country, not as enemies. I am counting on that, as well as the rapid pace of our military operations, to cause their insurgency to collapse before it gains permanence."

"There were regrettable incidents in the fighting by irregulars in the West," Lee acknowledged. "It is well that we put a stop to those. It is bad enough that this must be a war between brothers. When it is over we must have a peace between brothers."

"A peace between brothers!" exclaimed McClellan. "We must have it. The country is tired of fanaticism. It is tired of John Brown's Raid to free slaves in Virginia and Bill Yancey's Raid to kidnap free Negroes in Michigan. Let us have a just war to reclaim our errant Northern brothers followed by a just peace that will establish the Confederate Union

176

as a unified republic, not a make-believe country constantly at war with itself. I have lost my young friend Elmer Ellsworth --- who was also Mr. Lincoln's young apprentice --- and I will lose friends on both sides if this war continues. I want it to stop now. I never again want to draw my sword against my fellow Americans."

"President Douglas has been talking about that too," said Davis. "It's tearing him up inside having to be fighting his friends in the North like Lincoln and Seward --- who was also very kind to me during my illness. It tears at my heartstrings too. We must convince the Free Staters that the Confederate Union is their country as well as ours. Aleck Stephens says we must be prepared to make concessions on slavery."

"Didn't he just say that slavery is the cornerstone of our civilization?" asked Lee.

"He wants to strengthen slavery by reforming it," Davis explained. "He wants to make it less objectionable to the Free States by recognizing marriage and family relations so slave families can't be broken up and sold separately. He wants to allow Negroes to be educated. He says both races will make faster progress if the conditions of slavery are liberalized."

"To tell the truth, that is consistent with my own thinking," confessed Lee. "The world is modernizing. Slavery must modernize. If it remains rigid the institution may fracture. Make it flexible enough to change with the times and it will thrive."

"It will become easier after we've suppressed the Rebellion," added McClellan. "I have always felt that Southerners would become more progressive in managing your Negroes if the Abolitionists were not always hurling insults in your faces. Once the Abolitionists are suppressed you will be able to decide for yourselves how to reform the institution."

"It seems our business for today is satisfactorily concluded," affirmed Davis. "I expect General Lee would like to get back to Arlington in time for dinner with his family. He must have a full day's rest before going into the field. Tomorrow let's take our breakfast together at the White House and have a final discussion of our operations. Then we can escort General Lee to the train waiting to take him to Gettysburg. I hope President Douglas will be well enough to see you off, General."

There came a knock. Adjutant General Cooper escorted Secretary of State Horatio Seymour into the room.

"Gentlemen," Seymour said with a tear staining his face, "I have just come from the White House. I have the tragic duty to inform you that President Douglas has passed away. Vice President Jefferson Davis will please accompany me to the Capitol to be sworn in as President of the Confederate Union."

26

Cleveland, July 20, 1861

Maybe Stephen Douglas has got the best of it. He has mercifully passed away before having to bear the dreadful burdens that are coming.

President Abraham Lincoln wept as he looked out the window of the Hargreaves Mansion, now rented on the United Free States' account as the President's Residence. He wept over the death of the man who had become his enemy in war! But Lincoln could never bring himself to think of Stephen Douglas as an enemy, not after a lifetime of interwoven destinies with qualities of mutual admiration and even friendship along with its acrimony and rivalry.

He wept for many more than Douglas. His wife's sister Frannie and her husband were among the thousands killed in the savage partisan fighting in Springfield and many other towns along the Free States' military frontier. His young friend Elmer Ellsworth was gone, one of the first to die liberating the captive Negroes at Delphi. Captain Nathaniel Lyon had been killed the day before yesterday fighting to the end against the Confederates besieging the Free Staters in St. Louis.

And now a telegram had arrived from Pennsylvania's Governor Curtin. Curtin reported that former Provisional President Fremont, who had impetuously set off with a volunteer militia regiment for Pennsylvania, had been wounded while leading an attack against Confederates at a place called Gettysburg. Curtin's telegram said a full report was on the way by courier.

Heshook his head at Fremont's reckless risking of his life. Then he smiled at Fremont's gallantry.

Our bravest officers seek to prove their worth by displaying their valor under fire, but what a price it extracts from them! Elmer Ellsworth's valor cost him his life at Delphi. Captain Lyon died defending St. Louis. And now Fremont is wounded. This war is bound to kill and maim the most gallant men of this generation.

Beyond the loss of life and property, he lamented the destruction of the nation's spirit. The old United States as a single sovereignty founded on the principle that "all men are created equal" was gone. The bulk of its former territory, administered now by the Confederate Union, was dedicated to the principle that "for some men to enslave others is a sacred right of self government." The Northeastern Free States, if they could resist conquest by the Confederate Union, would become a diminished incarnation of the great libertarian republic founded by Jefferson, Washington, Adams, Madison, Franklin, and Hamilton.

His speculative mind, which often sought to peer into the future, wandered there at this moment. His mind's eye saw the looming shadow of the next century, an age of fantastic new developments in machinery, railroads, telegraphs, and who knew what other inventions of Man's fertile intellect.

He perceived that the heart of North America, larger and potentially more productive than every European Power combined, would grow fantastically during the coming century. Its present population of thirty million would grow tenfold. The metropolis of New York would be duplicated a hundred times and more. The development of industry would multiply the wealth of the continent, making it the first power of the earth. Would the North American nations emerging from this war become great powers for spreading liberty among Mankind, or agents of oppression?

A thought crystalized in his mind. *We were right to declare our Independence from the Confederate Union! We had no place in a country that has regressed so far from our founding principles. The age of machinery is looming. The age of slavery is passing. Let us fight to our last breath for our Independence. Even if we should be conquered in the end and*

180

forced to submit to the government of the Confederate Union, then at least we will have shown the world that we were willing to fight and die defending the principle that all men are destined to be free!

He decided to waste no more time lamenting the dead. He must devote his full energies to cyphering how to preserve the Free States' independence. The most immediate threat was the Confederate Union's armies gathering on the frontiers. Next came the financial disorder following the loss of most of the Free State's gold reserves and its access to financial companies in New York. He would have to expedite Treasury Secretary Salmon Chase's plan to finance the new government with bond issues and paper currency; otherwise, the Free States' military effort would surely falter if its economy could no longer conduct business.

Then there were diplomatic considerations. Secretary of State Seward advised him to ask for a commercial treaty with Great Britain. The loss of the great port and rail nexus around New York City made it essential for the Free States to obtain the right of tariff-free transit of the St. Lawrence and the Canadian railroads above the Great Lakes to maintain trade and military communication between New England and the Inland States. The Confederate Union could be expected to blockade Boston and the New England ports, leaving the St. Lawrence as the Free States' only outlet to the world.

Seward expected that in return for offering the Free States transit of the St. Lawrence and the Canadian railroads connecting it to the Great Lakes, the British would ask for the cession of New Hampshire and Maine above Latitude 45 to connect their Canadian railroad hub at Montreal to an ice-free port on the Atlantic.

Should I begin our War of Independence by asking the Congress to authorize a treaty ceding part of our territory to Great Britain?

Before everything else came the military emergency. The eminent loss of St. Louis would soon release thousands of Missouri and Southern Illinois militiamen to reinforce the Confederate Union's army in Central Illinois. The other crucial point was Philadelphia, linked to the Free States by one rail line to the west and a circuitous route to the north. If these communications were broken, Philadelphia would have to be surrendered.

Lincoln's Cabinet was divided on whether to evacuate what they could of Philadelphia's population, industry, and financial assets to the capital here in Cleveland; or to stake the Free State's fortunes on sending enough men in to hold the city and its railroad communications. In the West they were undecided on whether to distribute their available forces along the military frontier through Illinois and Indiana or to mass the bulk of their newly minted recruits around Chicago to strike a counterblow after the Confederate Unionists committed themselves to an attack.

He made two quick decisions. First, the Free States would stake their fortunes on holding Philadelphia.

If we evacuate the city, a spirit of defeatism will radiate outward to demoralize our forces everywhere. Our men will surrender every other point without a fight. We must declare our intention to hold Philadelphia, and then we must do whatever we must to hold it, even if that means throwing in every available man from Ohio eastward.

Next, he decided to endorse Sam Grant's view of distributing his forces along the military frontier in Indiana and Illinois. Grant had told him that if any part of that line came unhinged, the entire line would fail. It could only be reestablished, if at all, along the Kankakee and upper Wabash river valleys a hundred miles further north. That, too, would cause an unacceptable loss of territory and morale.

I do not know Grant, but I must trust his judgment, based on his recovery of Central Illinois during the partisan fighting.

Above everything else, he needed to inspire the people to fight on, through whatever setbacks and casualties might come. But what could be said to inspire them now? St. Louis was about to be lost after a six-week battle. Lyon's men had made the Confederates pay dearly for every street, house, and commercial building in the city --- a valorous sacrifice, but perhaps not the kind of "victory" to fully inspire the people.

As he was thinking on this, his young secretary John Hay walked in, a jaunty spring in his step. He was always cheered by Hay, a perennial optimist who kept up to date on the latest news, often learning of events before he did.

"What 'glad tidings' do you bring today, Mister Hay?"

"News from Pennsylvania sent by the courier you were expecting from Governor Curtin. The courier is ordered to deliver his message to you personally."

Lincoln motioned for Hay to send in the courier, who turned out to be Governor Curtin's private secretary. Lincoln asked him to spend the night and carry back his response to Governor Curtin in the morning. He asked Hay to show the courier to the guest bedroom and have the cooks prepare his supper. He tore open the packet. The first thing that fell out was *The Harrisburg Patriot:*

VICTORY AT GETTYSBURG!

On Wednesday July 17th, John C. Fremont's Regiment of Ohio volunteers surprised and routed a Confederate Union force gathering at Gettysburg. Over one hundred of the enemy were killed, over three hundred wounded, and upward of one thousand captured so far. Thousands more of the enemy scattered like rats in all directions, as fast as their legs would carry them. Confederate General Robert E. Lee was last reported fleeing ignominiously towards Hanover.

Our loss was less than one hundred killed and wounded. Our gallant Colonel of Militia John C. Fremont was counted among the wounded, being unhorsed by shot and shell as he routed the Confederates from the field.

While the Confederates were pretending to attack Philadelphia from the directions of New York City and Wilmington, Fremont's aggressive scouting unmasked their true intent of capturing the City of Liberty by way of Harrisburg. *That* fantastic scheme has been consigned to the Confederates' wastepaper basket!

Three cheers for the gallant Fremont and his dashing Free State men!

After the newspaper came the letter from Governor Curtin.

Dear Mr. President:

The Hon. John C. Fremont, upon completing his office as Provisional President of our General Government, arrived here and presented himself to me. He arrived with the regiment of Ohio volunteers serving as his personal bodyguard. He brought with him specie to equip the majority of his men with mounts. He requested an appointment as "Colonel of Ohio Volunteers fighting for the Free State of Pennsylvania."

I made the appointment, we being very short of men to guard Harrisburg and the rail line running through it from Pittsburgh to Phildel. Fremont requested permission to scout with his men in the direction of Gettysburg, where citizens had reported the arrival of men wearing the insignia of the Confederate Union government. It is believed this was the vanguard of an advance toward Phildel. by way of Harrisburg.

Fremont struck this force gathering at Gettysburg and drove it from the field. The town is restored to our possession. The enemy's losses reported in yesterday's paper continue to rise as our men drive the Confederates out of Pennsylvania.

Colonels George Gordon Meade and John Reynolds have moved their men out of Phildel. and through Harrisburg and Wrightsville. Both are now across the Susquehanna and advancing to meet Fremont's command. It is hoped that the enemy in large numbers will be cut off and captured.

Our losses remain light. Our most serious loss was Fremont, whose arm was broken by a shell splinter. He is being tended by my doctor here in the Executive Mansion. He is expected to make a full recovery.

The courageous Colonel Fremont and his gallant Ohioans have earned our fullest measure of gratitude for thwarting the enemy's scheme. He may well have saved our State and our Cause. If you can spare any other men please send them. Rest assured that we will do our part to defend the Cradle of Liberty.

Governor Andrew Curtin

Executive Mansion, Harrisburg, Penna.

Even allowing for the possibility of exaggeration, it seemed a substantial victory was in the making. Meade and Reynolds must have brought their men west from Philadelphia with extraordinary rapidity and hit the Confederates fleeing Fremont's attack from the other direction. Absent Fremont's initiative the Confederates might have taken Harrisburg and gone on into Philadelphia, dooming the Free State hold on Pennsylvania. With Pennsylvania lost, the rest of the Free States would have folded.

What a blessing that Fremont was not elected Permanent President. In his reconnaissance to Gettysburg, he has done more to preserve the Free States than he might ever have done as President. I must inspire all our men to fight as he and his Ohioans have done at Gettysburg. I must persuade the Douglas voters that it is their fight too. I must inspire those hundreds of thousands in New York City who are going about their business in presumed neutrality to join our cause. I must try to persuade the moderate men in the Confederate Union that it is not in their best interests to support a war to snuff out our Independence.

He'd been searching for words for a great speech of inspiration ever since notified of his selection as President. The words began to crystalize in his mind. He wrote them down:

Four score and several years ago our fathers brought forth, upon this continent, a new nation, conceived in Liberty and dedicated to the proposition that all men are created equal.

Now we are engaged in a Second War of Independence, testing whether that nation or any nation so conceived and so dedicated may long endure. We are met on a battlefield of that war guarding the approaches to the Cradle of Liberty where that nation was conceived. We have come to honor those who here gave their lives so that the Lamp of Liberty lit by our fathers will endure.

We may be certain that our dedication to the principles of 1776 will be tested as surely today as they were tested then. They were tested at Delphi, as surely as at Lexington and Concord. They were tested here again at Gettysburg as surely as at Bunker Hill. Now, as then, the embattled citizens of a Free Republic stood their ground and turned back the armies sent forth by the tyrant to conquer them.

*We may be certain that we have the **means** to secure our independence::*

We are superior in numbers of free citizens to the Slave States styling themselves the Confederate Union. We far surpass them in manufactories and agricultural productions. We have a preponderance of mechanics, industrial workers, railroad engineers, and men possessing all the other inventive skills that modern warfare requires.

We are the Forge of Liberty.

Know that we do not fight alone. The Friends of Liberty in all parts of the world hear us, as they heard us in 1776.

Know that we are heard on a higher plane, by that Providence that never failed our fathers. Does any thoughtful man question whether Providence destines men to be slaves or to be free? Our Founders answered that question for us: "All men are endowed by their Creator with certain inalienable rights."

Let us now dedicate ourselves to the great tasks remaining before us: of liberating New York and reopening our Gateway to the World; of restoring the territorial integrity of our Free States; of liberating the Free States on the Pacific Coast that are held by the carry-overs of pro-slavery territorial governments; and of re-establishing our authority over the Free Territories of the West.

And after vindicating our independence by war, let us vindicate by our example that freedom is the natural condition of men. If we succeed in establishing our independence upon those principles, our late fellow citizens now residing under the government they call 'The

185

Confederate Union' may one day choose to join us in freedom rather than insist upon coercing us to join them in slavery.

If we shall continue to do that which we have already shown we **can** do, here on this battlefield and elsewhere, then this new nation, under God, shall carry forth its birthright of freedom --- so that government of the people, by the people, and for the people shall not perish from the earth.

This story is continued in *Confederate Union Volumes II, III, and IV:*

www.amazon.com/dp/B00AKG0LZI/

www.amazon.com/gp/product/B00GLHV8IY/

www.amazon.com/dp/B00RC08EBS/

www.amazon.com/dp/B07J3NGCFD/

Feedback: alsnewideas@gmail.com

About the Author

"Understanding history is a key to understanding the present and extrapolating the future."

- Alan Sewell

I've devoted my life to analyzing historical and current events and applying their historical lessons to today's business and economic issues.

Although every day is a new day, the new days are layered on top of repeating cycles of history as old as Mankind. The more we understand the cycles of history, the more complete will be our understanding of the present.

My writing is focused on American History, starting with the Civil War --- the crucible that forged us into a united country under one flag, with a preeminent and indivisible national government.

I have intensively studied the Civil War, especially its politics and political dissent. Having lived in Alabama, Georgia, Florida, Ohio, Kentucky, Illinois, New York, and Michigan, I understand how the conflict is seen from both sides of the Ohio River. I grew up close to the Civil War because my mother, raised in Georgia in the 1930's, knew aging Civil War veterans who fought for the South. Four of them were her great-grand-fathers. My father's family were Appalachian Unionists from North Alabama. Discussions about the war were lively in our family.

I have written two articles for the December 1981 *Civil War Times Illustrated Special issue: DISSENT: FIRE IN THE REAR.* These articles chronicle the dissent of the Unionist minority in North Alabama against the Confederacy, and dissent by Illinois Copperheads against President Lincoln's government. I have also reviewed books in CWTI on the Pennsylvania Antiwar Movement and the career of General John Logan in Illinois.

Feedback: alsnewideas@gmail.com

Other Books by Alan Sewell

August 23, 1864: The Day Abraham Lincoln Won the Civil War chronicles the most critical day of the war:

https://www.amazon.com/dp/B07M6HZR48/

"Short and very sweet, this book leaves a most pleasurable aftertaste; it is as though Lincoln conversed with you."

Abraham Lincoln began the morning of August 23, 1864 by despairing of re-election:

"This morning, as for some days past, it seems exceedingly probable that this Administration will not be re-elected. Then it will be my duty to so co-operate with the

President elect (George McClellan, running on the Peace Platform), as to save the Union between the election and the inauguration; as he will have secured his election on such ground that he cannot possibly save it afterwards."

The Union was losing as many as 15,000 men killed, crippled, and dead from disease per week. Men up to the age of 45 were being conscripted to fill the gaping holes. Many deserted or surrendered at the first opportunity. Officers who had turned Lee back at Gettysburg last year had been killed or discharged with wounds. Incompetents and drunkards took their places. Grant's army was suffering staggering defeats at battles it would have won in previous years.

Robert E. Lee's Confederate army was not only holding fast in Virginia, but had recently raided the outskirts of Washington, taking Mr. Lincoln under fire. On August 23rd bad news poured in from all fronts. Lincoln's friends warned him he would not be re-elected. George McClellan, a pre-war protege of Jefferson Davis, would be the next president.

During the course of the day, Mr. Lincoln made a series of decisions that swung the balance back in his favor and enabled him to prevail in November's election, thus seeing the war through to Union victory.

This is the story of that day.

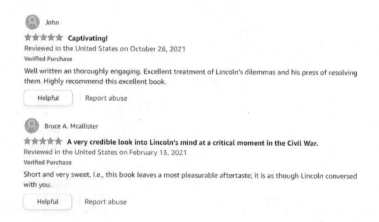

Fire in the Heartland is another novelized true story that tells the hidden stories of the Civil War of political intrigues behind the lines that decided the outcome of the Civil War as much as did its battles.

https://www.amazon.com/Fire-Heartland-Civil-story-youve-ebook/dp/B00514WNYG/

FIRE IN THE HEARTLAND

Fire in the Heartland: A Civil War Novel of the Decision that Won the Civil War Kindle Edition

by Alan Sewell ▾ (Author) ▾ | Format: Kindle Edition

★★★★☆ ▾ 7 ratings

See all Formats and editions

Kindle	Paperback
$0.00 kindleunlimited	$21.75

An untold story

FIRE IN THE HEARTLAND is a novelized true story that fills in the gaps of our knowledge about little-known events that decided the outcome of the Civil War. It provides a unique insight into the personal and political intrigues that were part of the war. And it's a great read.

- Fire in the Heartland gives us a different perspective on the Civil War. As a career military officer, I saw Generals McClellan, Grant, Sherman, Jackson, Lee and others portrayed in different lights. I saw how close Lincoln came to losing reelection and how close McClellan came to winning the Presidency. Had that happened, our nation today would look very different.

- Fire in the Heartland takes the reader into the levels of the War that are seldom seen...the depth of the political intrigue has always needed to be exposed and is done quite interestingly and provocatively.

- I must say that I both enjoyed the book, and learned much by reading it, and I, a former history teacher, recommend it highly.

Of a decision that won the Civil War

By Alan Sewell on Amazon

I've also been commended for "interpreting the American experience" into critical watersheds when political and economic crises were resolved to advance the country into the next era of its history. These pivot points of American history are analyzed in ***The Diary of American Exceptionalism:***

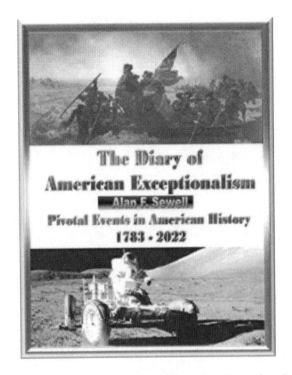

"If we could first know where we are, and whither we are tending, we could better judge what to do, and how to do it."

So said Abraham Lincoln as he contemplated the great issues of containing slavery and preserving the Union. This book is written to show where we are, and whither we may be tending, by explaining our current political controversies in the context of where we have been at similar crisis points in the past.

As this book is being updated for the 2022 Edition, our political controversies have intensified beyond what most Americans would have believed possible even a few years ago. The founding principles and history of our country are denigrated by many grating voices of elites in academia, media, elected officials, and government bureaucracies. Some say they are fearful of maintaining our democratic forms of government.

Yet we remain the essential, exceptional nation, a continent-wide republic of ambitious and outspoken free people. If we are more boisterous than people in other countries, it is because we inherited the traditions of generations of free people accustomed to making their voices heard. This book is written as a distilled essence of American history, explained in the words of the people who made it. It focuses narrowly but intensively on six periods of quantum change that moved us into new political and economic directions. Since it appears we may be at another turning point in our history, it may provide insights into our future direction.

I want readers to experience these crises as living history, the way people who lived through them did before they knew the outcomes of their decisions. We should seek to understand their optimistic visions of success, and their pessimistic fears of defeat, during our existential crises. They were human beings like the rest of us, prone to moments of despair. They could have surrendered the United States to mediocrity and failure. However, they understood that our country had been founded with an exceptional destiny, that they saw as their highest duty to preserve.

When President Lincoln spoke at Gettysburg, he said the Union Government must prevail so that "government of the people, by the people, for the people, shall not perish from the earth." His State of the Union message was: "We shall nobly save or meanly lose the last best hope of earth." He believed that democracy is a national treasure we hold in trust for all mankind.

During the depths of the Great Depression President Franklin Delano Roosevelt also reminded us of our exceptional spiritual and material prosperity:

"There is a mysterious cycle in human events. To some generations much is given, of other generations much is expected. This generation of Americans has a rendezvous with destiny." And "We shall fulfill...the apparent Utopia which Jefferson imagined for us in 1776."

Now we are in the depths of another crisis of the American spirit, when it has become fashionable in elitist circles to ridicule the traditional values we deem "American." I first heard these sentiments expressed during the 1960s when our society was torn by chaos that bordered on revolution. This turbulent time I experienced while coming of age is captured in this video collage by Chuck Braverman in 1968:

www.youtube.com/watch?v=vtz5Emyldwg

We heard phrases like "the next civil war, revolution, resistance, democracy is under threat, America is in decline." We emerged from that trauma, repaired the damage, and emerged stronger. Now, much later in my life, we have entered another turbulent period of chaos, repudiation of traditional values, and breakdown of society. A third of Americans seek to shift our politics to the Populist Right, a third seeks the Progressive Left, and a third desires to maintain the status quo. This book focuses on the five previous critical periods of our history that reshaped the country, and relates them to the sixth we are now experiencing:

Fragmentation — Federalism — Union (1783-1815) was our first existential crisis testing whether we would squander our Independence by fragmenting into warring factions, thereby allowing most of our territory to be reabsorbed back into the British, French, and Spanish empires. Ultimately, our Founders' vision of a continent-spanning Republic, governed by democratic principles, prevailed.

Secession — War — Nationalism (1858-1867) tested whether we were a Union of sovereign states free to resume their independence at will, or a union of individuals under a sovereign national government superior to the states.

Wealth — Depression — Empire (1890-1900) After the Civil War, the United States developed our industrial economy while advancing the frontier to the Pacific Coast. However, the development was not sustainable. We suffered our first great depression in 1894-1897. Unemployment, hunger, and rioting disrupted our cities and required suppression by the army. We became aware that a modern urban / industrial economy

195

develops instabilities requiring moderation by government. However, the reform agendas of that era were short-circuited by the fever for overseas expansion, that took us far beyond our North American homeland and made us a global power.

Wealth — Depression — Liberalism (1929-1934). Our economy revived and generally prospered between 1900 and 1929. It took on its modern look and feel with production of automobiles, appliances, national radio broadcasts, the mass migration of farm workers to cities, and the migration of city people to suburbs. Then it all came crashing down in 1929 due to an imbalance between production and consumption. Franklin Roosevelt's New Deal rebalanced the economy by bolstering consumption and tamping back excess investment in production and unsound speculation in financial assets.

Chaos — Humiliation — Conservatism (1968-1980). The 1960s were destined to be chaotic. Social unrest at home, a deteriorating economy, and our failure to defeat the communists in South Vietnam, led many to believe the United States was in decline. The election of Ronald Reagan, who campaigned on free market principles, revived our economy, and remade much of the world in our image. We also put our values fully into practice at home by ending racial segregation and discrimination and granting full civil rights to our African American citizens.

Globalism — Great Recession — {Populism or Progressivism?}: (2008-2020) Some "Cycles of History" historians believe we are entering a sixth pivot point, as demonstrated by the rise of unconventional new candidates on the Populist Right and Progressive Left. We may be able to discern our future direction by comparing this period to previous pivot points in our history.

This book has been researched over a 40-year period. It began with primary sources at the libraries of Georgia Tech, Emory University, and Case Western University, going back to 1800. Three articles derived from the research have been purchased by leading popular history magazines. It has been updated with current events, including the elections of 2016 and 2020. It is important now more ever to have a full-spectrum perspective on American History, to understand how our exceptional destiny as the beacon of liberty and opportunity for Mankind overcame the oppressive aspects of our history and in much of the world beyond our borders. The most widely excerpted passage from this book is a remark by George Washington in 1787:

The national government, he said, would have to reconcile the conflicts between the commercial North and the agricultural South and mediate between the minds of men "accustomed to acting and thinking differently." Americans must learn "to distinguish between oppression and the necessary exercise of lawful authority, to discriminate the spirit of liberty from that of licentiousness."

Here we are, after 235 years, still trying to mediate between the minds of Americans accustomed to thinking and acting differently and threading the needle between the spirit of liberty and licentiousness.

Made in the USA
Columbia, SC
06 February 2023

11897411R00119